"Let me go," she squeaked out, struggling to pry herself from the powerful arms restraining her.

She attacked with her elbow, eliciting a grunt from her attacker.

"Damn it, Morgan. It's me."

She froze at the familiar gruff voice.

No, it couldn't be him. Maybe she really had gone crazy. Because no way could he actually be here.

Maybe she was hallucinating this entire exchange.

But nope, there he was, all six-feet, three-inches of him. The familiar broad shoulders, the muscles rippling beneath his hunter-green sweater. The scent of spice and aftershave she knew so well.

Releasing a heavy sigh, Quinn crossed his arms over his firm chest and said, "I knew I'd find you here."

After a few seconds of silence, Morgan finally gave up on attempting speech.

Instead, she let out a shaky breath and threw her arms around the only man she'd ever truly loved.

Dear Reader,

My favorite types of romances have always been
reunion stories. Whether it's betrayal or distance
or simply growing apart, I enjoy watching a couple
overcome past issues and find their way back to each
other. In *Her Private Avenger,* Morgan and Quinn have a
rocky past, but their powerful love for each other hasn't
died in the two years they were apart.

And of course, there's nothing that brings an estranged
couple closer together than a hefty dose of danger.
I've always been a fan of those cold-case shows on
television, so I decided it would be interesting to give
my heroine a decade-old cold case to solve. Throw
in a hero that will do anything to protect her, and
you've got a story packed with tender emotion
and a lot of suspense!

I hope you enjoy Morgan and Quinn's story! I'm
always happy to hear from readers, so visit my website,
www.ellekennedy.com, and drop me a line.

Happy reading!

Elle Kennedy

ELLE KENNEDY

Her Private Avenger

ROMANTIC
SUSPENSE

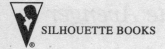

SILHOUETTE BOOKS

ISBN-13: 978-0-373-27704-9

HER PRIVATE AVENGER

Recycling programs
for this product may
not exist in your area.

Printed in U.S.A.

Books by Elle Kennedy

Silhouette Romantic Suspense

Silent Watch #1574
Her Private Avenger #1634

ELLE KENNEDY

Elle Kennedy grew up in the suburbs of Toronto, Ontario, and holds a B.A. in English from York University. From an early age, she knew she wanted to be a writer, and actively began pursuing that dream when she was only a teenager. When she's not writing, she's reading. And when she's not reading, she's making music with her drummer boyfriend, oil painting or indulging her love for board games.

Elle loves to hear from her readers. Visit her at her website www.ellekennedy.com, or stop by her blog, http://sizzlingpens.blogspot.com, to chat with Elle and fellow Harlequin writers.

To Diana Ventimiglia, for having faith in this story.
I'll miss you, D!

Chapter 1

"**I** don't like being summoned." Quinn leaned against the wide door frame and directed a withering look at the silver-haired man behind the desk.

"I don't like summoning you. And I certainly don't like needing your help." Edward Kerr's features grew pained, as if the admission caused him physical torture.

Intrigued, Quinn stepped into the spacious office, his black boots barely making a sound as he crossed the pristine parquet floor toward Kerr. A lone visitor's chair sat in front of the forbidding mahogany desk but he made no move to sit down. He didn't plan to stay long. In fact, he wasn't entirely sure why he showed up here to begin with. Two years ago he'd vowed never to lay eyes on this man—or his daughter—again. Why he'd broken that vow still eluded him.

He examined the older man's face, saw the worry flickering in Kerr's dark blue eyes, and his intrigue deepened. Revealing his weaknesses was not in Edward Kerr's character. His entire career could be credited to his ruthless nature, his ability to remain poised and controlled in any situation. Which raised the question—what was causing Kerr's obvious anxiety?

Or perhaps he should be asking *whom*.

"Morgan is in trouble," Kerr said, getting right to the point.

Something that resembled concern tugged at Quinn's gut. He managed to paste on a mask of indifference and said, "So?"

"That's your response? *So?*" Disbelief washed across the older man's face. "This doesn't worry you?"

"Worry suggests I actually give a damn about Morgan's well-being." He offered a cool smile. "I don't."

"You're lying."

Quinn crossed his arms over his chest. "Is this the reason you called me, to inform me that your daughter is in trouble? If so, you've wasted both our time."

A pleading note entered Kerr's gravelly voice. "I need you to help her."

He shook his head in irritation before taking two steps back toward the door. "Good night, Edward."

"Goddamn it, Quinn! She's in danger!"

Another step to the door. *Don't look back,* a little voice warned. *He's playing you. They're both playing you.*

"She's missing, Quinn."

A flicker of alarm. *Ignore it, keep walking.*

Almost at the doorway. One more step and he'd be out of here. Free of Edward Kerr. Free of Morgan. Free of the tornado of memories that assaulted him the moment he'd heard her name.

"She tried to kill herself last week."

That last revelation made him freeze. Before he could stop it, the image of Morgan's gorgeous face swept into the forefront of his brain. Her wavy blond hair, always haphazardly falling onto her regal forehead. Those perceptive blue eyes that tilted upward just enough to make her look exotic. The stubborn slant of her chin, the delicate earlobes she refused to pierce. Then he heard her voice in his head, her sassy no-nonsense tone, spoken in a throaty pitch that made her sound as if she walked around with a perpetual cold.

And he remembered her fire, her determination, her *will*.

Slowly, he turned to face the father of the woman he'd once desperately loved.

"Bull," he said flatly. "She would never try to take her own life."

"I'm telling the truth." Kerr's eyes became shuttered, but there was genuine conviction in his voice.

Then again, Kerr had always been a convincing liar. He'd manipulated the press for years, making them fall hook, line and sinker for his my-poor-mentally-ill-daughter spiel.

But Morgan wasn't crazy. Never had been. In fact, she was the strongest woman Quinn had ever met. She valued herself—her *life*—too damn much to throw it all away by… by what? He was even afraid to ask.

"She drove her car off a bridge," Kerr elaborated as if reading his mind.

His head jerked up. *"Pardon me?"* Once again he found himself meeting the other man's expressionless eyes.

"I know, it sounded unbelievable to me when the police called after they'd pulled her car out of the river. Apparently she was intoxicated. There are half a dozen witnesses who confirm she had several drinks before leaving the pub and getting into her car. Her brother was there, too. He said she was quite upset."

"Upset about what?"

"Layla Simms's body was discovered last week."

Quinn immediately recognized the name. Layla Simms was the young woman who'd gone missing nearly a decade ago, Morgan's best friend from high school.

"Where was the body found?" Quinn asked.

"Autumn." The older man sighed. "That poor family. I'd

heard Wendy and Mort Simms never gave up hope that their daughter was alive. This must have been quite a shock for them."

Quinn absorbed the information. Autumn was Morgan's hometown, which the Kerr family practically owned before Edward was elected into the United States Senate and moved away for bigger and better things. The Kerrs relocated to D.C. a few years after the Simms girl's disappearance, Quinn recalled. But Morgan had always been convinced Layla had been killed and that her body lay somewhere in the idyllic town they'd grown up in. She went back there at least twice a year to rustle a few trees and see if any answers fell out, but they never did. Quinn once asked her why she kept going back, kept searching for something she might never find, and she'd always replied with, "She's there, Quinn. I know it."

Well, apparently Morgan had been right.

He felt a startling sense of pride that Morgan had known the truth all along, but he quickly tamped it down and tried to focus on the other startling aspects of this conversation.

"Morgan went back there when she heard the body was found?" he asked curtly.

Kerr made an exasperated sound. "You know my daughter, so stubborn about this old case. She went to the memorial service, then stayed to *investigate*."

The condescension in the senator's tone made Quinn's gut tighten. "We both know she's a damn good journalist," he said. "She's perfectly capable of solving that case."

Why was he defending her, damn it? Quinn quickly reined in the response, pasted an aloof expression on his face and added, "So did she come up with any leads?"

"We're getting off track," Edward said, suddenly looking frazzled. "This isn't about the Simms girl. This is about Morgan attempting suicide."

Suicide was the last word he'd ever expect to associate with

Morgan. Had she changed so much in the two years since he'd walked out on her? With that question came a stab of guilt.

She betrayed you.

He held on to that thought, forcibly pushing the guilt out of his body. Whatever Morgan's state of mind these past couple of years, he was not at fault. He'd had good reason to walk away from her. Damn good reason.

"She was under psychiatric observation at a private clinic outside the city," Kerr continued. "And last night—"

"You had her *committed?*"

"—she escaped," the other man finished, paying no attention to Quinn's incredulous interruption.

"Escaped? For God's sake, don't tell me you were keeping her under restraint."

"It was for her own good," Kerr snapped. "She's a danger to herself. I'd never be able to live with myself if something happened to my only daughter."

Quinn snorted. "Right, because Morgan's best interests have always been your first priority."

"I've always tried to protect her," Kerr shot back. "Especially from herself. You know what she's like, constantly landing into trouble. The tabloid photos, the arrest…my PR team worked around the clock trying to repair her image."

"She was a teenager who just lost her mother. Of course she acted out. What'd you expect her to do, sit at home and knit?"

The senator's blue eyes flashed. "I expected her to act responsibly."

Lord, why was he still here? Looking at Kerr's irritating face, listening to him spew the usual bull about his trouble-maker daughter, Quinn was tempted to march right out the door. But one thing was stopping him.

"Where is she now?" he asked gruffly.

"I don't know," Kerr said, "but I need you to find her. I don't trust anyone else with the task."

His lips curled in a sneer. "Funny, you never trusted me before."

Kerr uncharacteristically slammed one hand against the desk. "This has nothing to do with the past, damn it. You have to find her."

"I'll think about it." He sounded like a callous bastard and he knew it. Yet he couldn't ignore the anger and bitterness yanking at his gut. He'd lost the woman he loved because of this man.

"I understand your anger and reluctance." Kerr swallowed. "But you simply have to find her, Adam."

Adam. Shit. Now there was a name he hadn't heard in years.

"You can pretend all you want," the other man added, "but we both know you still care for her. And you might be a bastard, but you'd never walk away knowing Morgan might be in danger."

Quinn swore under his breath. He loathed this man. Loathed Kerr's manipulation and arrogance and those guilt cards he liked to throw out whenever it suited him.

But the son of a bitch was right.

No matter how bitter he was, no matter how angry and disappointed, if Morgan was in trouble, Quinn couldn't turn his back.

Not by a long shot.

The cabin was deserted and shrouded with darkness as Morgan Kerr let herself in with the spare key she'd found under the porch. Good thing she knew her way around, even in the shadows. During the walk here, as she navigated the dark, slushy woods in the direction of the snow-littered clearing where this little cabin stood, she'd wondered if the place would look the same. If it would *feel* the same. To the former, the answer was yes. The cabin's small living room still boasted a sofa with plaid upholstery and a coffee stain on the right arm, the gorgeous stone fireplace, the scratchy forest-green carpet.

But did it feel the same?

Not in the slightest.

Setting her purse on the table in the hallway, Morgan breathed in the scent of mothballs, dust and loneliness. Quinn obviously hadn't been back here since they'd parted ways, and every inch of the cabin ached with loss. As did her heart.

A part of her had been hoping she'd walk in and find him here. Big, hard body sprawled on the couch, dark hair messy as always, his piercing green eyes sparkling with love and desire.

God, she missed him.

Forget about Quinn. You've got bigger things to worry about.

She approached the sofa and sank onto the plump cushions, a hysterical laugh bubbling in the back of her throat then spilling out and breaking through the silence of the dark room. Oh, yeah, she definitely had bigger things to worry about.

Like the fact that everyone in her life thought she was crazy and suicidal.

Morgan released a long calming breath and lifted her knees up to her chest, wrapping her arms around them. She didn't care what her father or Tony or those doctors said. She hadn't purposely driven her car off a bridge.

Someone had run her off the road.

Pain seized her insides as she remembered what her father had said when she told him what really happened. *You were just imagining things. You were drunk and upset and not thinking clearly. Nobody tried to kill you, Morgan.*

The pain transformed into anger when she thought about the staff at the psychiatric hospital her dad had her committed to. The nurses' sympathetic stares. The doctor's patronizing words. And her father's voice, drifting in from the hallway as he spoke to the doctor.

My daughter is…ill. She's suffered with delusions and mood swings all her life.

Delusions and mood swings, her ass. Sure, she'd been rebellious as a teenager, but that didn't make her nuts. And was it her fault the press had decided to paint her with the troublemaker brush? *Senator's Wild Child. Senator's Daughter Caught with Cocaine. Senator's Loony Daughter.*

The memory of all those newspaper headlines had her clenching her fists in fury. She'd never deserved all those labels, and yet somehow she'd gotten stuck with them, and she'd been spending the past ten years trying to rid herself of the stigma.

She'd been doing so well, too. Out of the tabloids for years, landed a legitimate job at a respectable magazine, used a pseudonym to build her writing reputation.

And now…now she was back to square one.

A wave of frustration crashed into her, causing her to stand abruptly. A plan. She needed a plan. She couldn't hide out in this cabin forever, no matter how safe she felt here. No matter how close it made her feel to Quinn.

If she was going to find the answers, then she needed to return to the scene of the crime.

Autumn. It started in Autumn.

And that's where she needed to be.

The frustration eased, replaced with a rush of determination that coursed through her blood and got her adrenaline going. She was *not* suicidal or crazy.

There had been another car on the bridge that night. She'd *seen* the headlights in her rearview mirror, *felt* the impact of the other vehicle's front bumper smashing into her car.

Which meant someone had tried to kill her.

And the only reason someone would've done that was because of Layla's disappearance. She'd been investigating her best friend's vanishing act for almost ten years, and the moment Layla's remains were found, someone pushed her car off a bridge? It was too much of a coincidence. In fact, it screamed cover-up.

Lifting her chin in resolve, she headed for the little table next to the front door, where she'd left the purse she'd retrieved from the drawer next to her hospital bed. The small leather bag contained her wallet, ID and credits cards, but she was loath to use anything other than cash in case her father had someone watching her accounts. Which he probably did. She knew he wanted her back in that psych ward, where the doctors could monitor her and make sure she didn't try to harm herself.

Her cell phone was mysteriously absent from her purse, but she could walk back to the gas station on the main road and call a taxi from there.

In the morning, she decided. She wasn't particularly keen on the idea of walking around in the dark, no matter how well she remembered these woods.

She dropped her purse on the table and headed back to the sofa. Then she froze.

Were those footsteps she'd just heard?

She swallowed hard, then focused on the soft noises coming from outside the cabin. *Snap, snap, snap.* Twigs snapping.

Probably an animal. A squirrel scurrying across the clearing, maybe a coyote in search of a midnight snack.

The noise grew louder, the distinct sound of footsteps climbing up the steps. The creak of the porch as the intruder approached the front door.

Her heart pounded against her rib cage, making it difficult to breathe, let alone think.

She needed a weapon. Her gaze darted wildly around the dark room, looking for anything she might be able to use in self-defense. She spotted the fireplace poker at the same time the doorknob began to turn.

Drawing in a breath, Morgan took a desperate step toward the fireplace but she was too late. The door swung open, more footsteps, and then someone grabbed her from behind.

"Let me go," she squeaked out, struggling to pry herself from the powerful arms restraining her. She attacked with her elbow, eliciting a grunt from her attacker.

"Damn it, Morgan. It's me."

She froze at the familiar gruff voice.

No.

No, it couldn't be him. Maybe she really had gone crazy. Because no way could he actually be here.

Heart pounding, she slowly turned to face the intruder, expecting to see a stranger, or hell, even air. Maybe she was hallucinating this entire exchange.

But nope, there he was, all six feet, three inches of him. The familiar broad shoulders, the muscles rippling beneath his hunter-green sweater. The scent of spice and aftershave she knew so well.

She blinked wildly, then studied his classically handsome features and piercing green eyes.

Oh, God, it was really him.

He was here.

Releasing a heavy sigh, Quinn crossed his arms over his firm chest and said, "I knew I'd find you here."

She opened her mouth to respond, but no words came out. Her pulse was drumming too loudly in her ears to formulate a sentence, her brain still trying to register the sight of him. After a few seconds of silence, Morgan finally gave up on attempting speech.

Instead, she let out a shaky breath and threw her arms around the only man she'd ever truly loved.

Chapter 2

Oh, lord, it felt good having her in his arms again. Heat coursed through Quinn's body, his pulse speeding up at the feel of Morgan's warm body against his, her soft hands clinging to his shoulders. Before he could stop himself, he inhaled the scent of her, the aroma of lavender he remembered far too well.

"Thank God you're here," she whispered, her breath tickling his neck.

It was the sound of her voice that snapped him out of the insanity. His body went stiff. Hands dropped from her waist. He took a step back, but waves of heat continued pulsing through his blood.

Quinn quelled the traitorous response and focused on Morgan's face. On those gorgeous eyes flickering with relief.

He wished she didn't look so good, but he hadn't expected anything less. Morgan had always been drop-dead gorgeous. Even now, looking a tad thin and more than a little pale, her beauty made his breath hitch. Her honey-blond hair was tied back in a ponytail that made her appear much younger than her twenty-eight years. She wore baggy jeans and a shapeless knit sweater, but Quinn knew underneath the clothing lay an endless supply of curves. The memory of her soft, womanly form was enough to send his pulse racing again, a reaction he neither appreciated nor welcomed.

"Are you okay?" he asked roughly, meeting her gaze.

"No." She emphasized the word by slowly shaking her head.

Obviously she was still honest to a fault, and her candid reply brought a reluctant smile to his lips. "I heard about the accident."

A flash of anger lit her eyes. "From my father?"

Quinn nodded.

Her lips tightened. "Let me guess. He's outside in the car, waiting for you to bring me out so the two of you could take me back to the hospital. Where I won't be able to *harm* myself."

Hurt and sarcasm dripped from each word. He saw that same hurt flickering on her face, and in that instant Quinn knew he'd been right. No way had Morgan tried to kill herself. He didn't give a damn what the senator thought. As usual, the man was dead wrong.

"Your father isn't outside. I came alone."

Morgan went silent for a moment, and then she shot him a shrewd look. "But he asked you to come."

"Yes."

She rolled her eyes as she drifted over to the couch and sank onto the cushions. "I wish I'd been there to hear him beg you to help."

He couldn't help a chuckle. "It was definitely a Kodak moment."

Morgan laughed softly. "I'll bet."

Okay. So this was easier than he thought it would be. They were talking, laughing, no awkward silences, no uncomfor—Oh, for Pete's sake, who was he kidding? This was difficult as hell, seeing Morgan after two years apart.

Stifling a sigh, he joined her on the sofa, sitting at the other end, and clasped his hands loosely on his lap. "Tell me about the accident," he finally said.

She raised one delicate eyebrow. "Wouldn't you rather we talk about the enormous pink elephant in the room first?"

"I have no idea what you're talking about."

"We haven't seen each other in two years, Quinn." Pain swarmed her eyes. "And the last time we were together, you told me to get out of your life and stay out."

He tried not to cringe. Damn, when she said it out loud, it sounded harsher than he remembered. But he'd been hurting like hell when he'd said those words.

"I probably could've been more diplomatic about it," he admitted ruefully.

She swallowed. "No. I deserved it."

As she'd always done when she was nervous or upset, Morgan nibbled on her bottom lip with her straight white teeth. Last time he'd seen her do it, she was telling him she wanted to postpone their wedding.

"So—" Morgan cleared her throat "—you've been neglecting this old place." She gestured around the cabin, the change of subject an obvious indication that she'd decided to go back to ignoring the pink elephant.

"I've been out of the country," he answered with a shrug.

He tried not to follow the sweep of her hands, not eager to focus too hard on his surroundings. This cabin had been their sanctuary, the place they'd gone to make love, where Morgan could avoid the scrutiny that came with being a senator's daughter.

In fact, it had been right here, on this couch, that Morgan first told him she loved him. He'd said it back, no hesitation—God, how he'd loved her—and proceeded to make passionate love to her. All night long.

The memory caused his gut to tighten. Damn it, he wasn't allowed to think about those days. He had no business remembering how it felt to kiss her, or make love to her. Or the sleepy smiles she used to give him when she woke up in his arms. Or the way she never backed down when she believed in something.

He gulped down a lump of bitterness. But she had backed down, hadn't she? When it really mattered, she'd allowed her father to talk her out of marrying him.

"Business going well?" she asked quietly.

"Yeah. Seems like everyone's getting themselves kidnapped these days. My guys and I did three extractions last month alone."

"Ah, the glorious life of a mercenary," she said wryly.

A short silence fell, and Quinn used the lull to gather up some courage. He knew what he had to do, and he knew exactly how Morgan would react. And damn, but he was in no shape to face off with her tonight. His chest felt raw, this reunion scraping him open and leaving his insides a mess.

"Quinn?"

He met her eyes. "Yeah?"

"What's bothering you?"

Now wasn't that a loaded question.

He ran a hand through his hair and steeled himself for a fight. "I'm just trying to decide whether we should head out tonight, or wait until morning."

Her hands dropped from her knees, fingers clenching into fists. "And where exactly would we be heading *to?*"

"I don't know. I'm assuming your father's house, or your apartment, if you'd prefer. Either way, I'm driving you back to the city."

Alarm washed over her features. "No! You can't take me there! My father will send me back to the psych ward."

Quinn fought a groan. She was right, of course. The second Edward had Morgan back, he'd commit her again.

But what was Quinn supposed to do about it? He'd promised Edward he would find Morgan, and he'd kept to his word. Here she was, safe and sound. Which meant it was time to get the hell out of this cabin. The memories were liable to suffocate him.

"Quinn, please, don't call my father." A pleading note entered her husky voice. "Give me some time to figure out what's going on."

"You just escaped from a psych ward. The senator's not going to let you run around and investigate."

Her blue eyes flashed. "Right, because I'll tarnish his precious image again. Well, I'm a journalist, Quinn, and I'm going to investigate no matter what my father says."

He didn't like the stubborn tilt of her chin. Once Morgan made up her mind about something…well, God help anyone who stood in her way.

Quinn opened his mouth to protest, but she startled him by slamming one hand down on the sofa cushions in an aberrant show of anger. "Someone tried to kill me, damn it!" she burst out.

Quinn's jaw tightened. "What are you talking about?"

"The night of the accident. Someone ran me off the bridge."

Cold fury clawed up his spine. The thought of anyone trying to harm her elicited a troubling pang of protectiveness. "Are you certain?"

"Of course," she said, sounding oddly defensive. "I saw headlights in my rearview mirror, and the next thing I knew, a car slammed into my bumper. The driver was a maniac, Quinn. Kept ramming into me, forced me into the guardrail and knocked me right over the edge."

"Did you tell the senator this?"

Pain filled her eyes. "He didn't believe me," she said flatly. "Said I was imagining it."

He muttered a soft curse. "That selfish bastard. He'd rather

have you look suicidal than be faced with a possible scandal."
He drew in a calming breath. "What do you remember about
the other car?"

She glanced at him in surprise. "You believe me?"

"Of course," he said softly. "You're many things, Morgan,
but suicidal isn't one of them."

A wave of relief crashed into Morgan's chest, making her
heart squeeze painfully. He believed her! After days of staring
into her dad's and brother's pitying eyes, she'd finally found
someone who didn't think she was a nut-job. Not that she
ought to be surprised. Quinn had always had the utmost faith
in her. When they first met, he'd laughed off all those tabloid
stories, telling her he didn't believe a word of them.

It was incredibly liberating knowing he still held that faith,
especially since it was glaringly obvious the last thing he
wanted to do was be here with her.

Since they'd sat down, those deep green eyes of his had
flickered with so many different emotions she had no clue
what to make of it. Bitterness had been prominent. A flash
of tenderness. Something that resembled sorrow. And when
you threw into the mix the longing, anger and desire she'd
also glimpsed, you got one confusing emotional cocktail.

She wanted to ask him if he hated her, but she couldn't
gather up enough courage to do it. Besides, did she really
want to know the answer?

"You honestly don't think I tried to kill myself?" she asked
instead, studying his expression.

Conviction laced his gruff voice. "Hell, no."

"Then don't tell my father you found me," she blurted
out.

"I can't do that, Morgan."

Something coiled in her belly. Irritation. Desperation,
maybe. And anger, because she was sick of everyone else
making decisions for her. Ever since the car accident—heck,
even before that—her father had been calling all the shots.

The only time she'd ever felt an inkling of freedom was when she and Quinn were together, but her father had managed to destroy that, too.

"Why not?" she demanded. "Just get in your car and forget you saw me. Or, here's a better idea, help me find out what the hell happened in Autumn."

She had no idea where the spontaneous request for help came from. She was a seasoned journalist, perfectly capable of investigating on her own. But that feeling of danger…it lingered in her gut like a stray animal, hounding at her. Quinn was a mercenary. He could protect her.

She glanced at his broad chest, the ripples of muscle straining against his sweater. A little thrill shot through her. She remembered with perfect clarity how it felt to run her fingers over that chest, the soft sound of pleasure he made when she pressed her lips to his—

No. Not going there.

She couldn't think about that right now, although from the sparks of heat going off like fireworks in her body, it was evident this man was still capable of eliciting a primal physical response in her. He'd always done that, made her hot and needy, just by being in the same room as her.

Looking oblivious to her painfully aroused state, Quinn's forehead creased with unease. "You're planning on going to Autumn." It was a statement, not a question.

"Yes."

"Bad idea," he said flatly.

She feigned innocence. "Why's that?"

Disapproval filled his eyes. "Someone ran you off a bridge. You go in asking questions, digging around, and you could end up asking the wrong person or digging in the wrong place."

"So come with me." She laughed derisively. "Keep me in line."

He responded with a laugh of his own, deep and genuine. "Keep you in line? That's like trying to teach a raging bull to do tricks." The laughter faded as rapidly as it came. "Forget it, Morgan. I'm not going to Autumn with you."

"Then I'll go alone."

He gave a firm shake of the head. "Only place you're going is home. Anything else is too dangerous."

She experienced a pang of disappointment, but rather than arguing, she dropped the issue. She knew the look in Quinn's eyes too well. He meant business. He wasn't going to help her. And she got the feeling he'd take her back to the city even if he had to drag her there, kicking and screaming.

"In fact," he continued, "we're leaving now."

"Couldn't we at least wait until morning?"

Something indefinable flashed across his face. Averting his eyes, he cleared his throat and said, "No. I don't have time to sit around here all night with you. We're leaving now."

She tightened her lips. "Fine."

His eyes narrowed. "Fine?"

"Yes, fine." She rose stiffly to her feet, tossing him a glance over her shoulder as she rounded the couch to get her purse. "Isn't that what you want?"

He stood up, arms crossed over that spectacular chest. "Yes, but it's not what you want. So why are you giving in so easily?"

She shrugged, and slung her purse over one shoulder. "We both know I'll be going to Autumn. This is just a small bump in the road. I broke out of the psych ward once. I can do it again."

"So that's your plan, dutifully come back with me and then escape again?"

"Yep."

He let out an exasperated breath. "You are the most stubb—" He stopped abruptly, suddenly frowning. "Forget it. Beggars can't be choosers. Your thoughtful compliance only makes my job easier. Once you're home, you'll be the senator's problem."

The sudden bite of hostility stung like hell, but she wasn't sure she blamed him. She'd hurt him when she'd canceled their wedding. Scratch that—*he'd* canceled their wedding. She'd simply asked to postpone it. But with Quinn, there was no such thing as a gray area. It was black and white, get married or don't. He'd chosen the latter.

Quinn moved to the door. "Get your coat. It's cold out there."

"I don't have a coat."

His eyes flashed. "You walked all the way here without a coat?"

She offered a stony look. "I was a little too focused on sneaking out of the *psychiatric* ward to worry about the weather."

He muttered something under his breath, then opened the door. They walked out to the rickety porch.

Quinn's back was to her as he locked up the cabin, and she took the opportunity to draw in a steady breath and examine the porch. Her heart skipped when she noticed a white ceramic flowerpot sitting on the wooden railing. About twice the size of a snow globe, but it would do the trick.

She had no intention of going back to D.C. tonight. She didn't think she could lose him during the hike to the car, but if she got a head start now...

"Don't forget to put this back," she said when he turned around. She stuck out her palm, and the silver spare key sparkled under the thin shaft of moonlight illuminating the front yard.

Without a word, he took the key and headed down the steps. Morgan followed him, casually picking up the empty flowerpot and tucking it behind her back. She waited until Quinn was on his knees, big body bent down to slip the key under the rock she'd liberated it from.

Another breath. Now or never.

Fighting the jolt of guilt that streaked through her, she lifted her arm and murmured, "I'm sorry."

Quinn's head swiveled sharply, but he had no time to react as the ceramic pot came crashing down on his head.

Chapter 3

Morgan took off running.

She didn't dare turn back to see if Quinn was following her but she knew she hadn't knocked him unconscious, as she'd hoped. No surprise. He'd always had a pretty thick skull. She'd heard his grunt of pain as the flowerpot connected with its target, the sound of ceramic splintering against his head, but he hadn't passed out. Still, she'd stunned him, and she suffered a tug of guilt as she tore through the woods.

She tried to ignore the image of Quinn's body falling backward from the impact. God, she hoped she hadn't hurt him. She wasn't a violent person, not usually anyway.

But she wasn't crazy, either, and she'd be damned if she was going to be forced back into that psych ward.

Twigs snapped under her sneakers as she ran, trees whipping by her face. Her cheeks grew flushed from the cold. She came dangerously close to slamming into a branch, but kept moving, slipping several times on the layer of slush beneath her feet.

Sucking in oxygen, she tried to pay attention to her surroundings, but she had no freaking clue where she was going. If she stopped for a minute and looked for her previous tracks, she'd be able to find her way back to the main road, but she couldn't risk it. No doubt Quinn was right behind her.

Keep going, she ordered herself. *Keep going. Keep go—*

She was suddenly jerked backward as a big hand yanked at her sweater from behind.

"Damn you!" came Quinn's infuriated voice.

He grabbed her shoulders and twisted her around, and the look in his eyes caused a lump of fear to lodge in her throat. She'd never seen him like this, his green eyes glittered with menace, his lips an angry slash across his face. She swallowed when she noticed the scrape on his left temple, the thin trail of blood on his cheek. He'd been cut when the pot had shattered. There were even little white pieces of ceramic caught in his dark hair. No wonder he looked like he wanted to throttle her.

His fury seemed to escalate when he caught sight of her face. "Don't!" he snapped. "Don't you dare be afraid of me."

"I—"

"A lot of things might have changed in two years, but not that. I would never hurt you. Never."

Her heart thudded against her rib cage, making each individual rib tremble. "I'm sorry," she murmured.

"For what?" he shot back. "Using my head like a piñata or thinking I was going to hit you just now?"

She cringed. "Both."

Quinn shook his head angrily. He looked like he was struggling to rein in his temper. "Damn it, Morgan. Do you think I want to be here right now? Do you think I enjoy chasing after you in the woods at midnight?"

"Then let me go," she begged him.

"I can't."

She heard the pain lining those two words, and when she

lifted her head to meet his gaze, her breath lodged in her throat. A kaleidoscope of emotions reflected back at her, the most prominent being sorrow. And then his eyes dropped to her mouth, and desire joined the mix.

She stared at him, transfixed, while a rush of pleasure poured into her body. He still wanted her. Oh, God, he still wanted her. The happiness she received from the realization was so strong she nearly keeled over backward. For two years she'd longed for this man, woken up in the middle of the night searching for his big, warm body. And in those two years, he hadn't contacted her. Not even once. She thought he'd gotten over her. That he'd somehow managed to exorcise the powerful attraction bonding them together.

It was unbelievably satisfying knowing he hadn't, that she wasn't alone in the longing department.

"Damn you," he said again, his voice thick.

"Quinn…" she began.

But he didn't let her finish. Even as her lips formed his name, his lips were swallowing up the sound. He captured her mouth, kissing her so deeply that all thoughts drained from her head. Common sense left her, too, as she kissed him back frantically. His lips were firm, his tongue hot and insistent as it slid into her mouth as if it belonged there. No, *because* it belonged there.

Morgan leaned into his hard body, angling her head for better access, drowning in his familiar kiss. As their mouths meshed and tongues tangled, she realized there would never be anyone else for her. She was his.

I missed you.

The words bit at her lips, so she kissed him back with more fervor, before those silly words could find a way out. But God, how she'd missed him. Missed *this*—his hot spicy taste, the way his five o'clock shadow deliciously scraped her cheek.

"Damn it."

His sudden curse jolted her from the haze of passion. She

gasped as he pulled back, the sensual contact snapping like a bungee cord.

Morgan looked up at him with wide eyes, her brain working so fast she feared it might shut down like an overloaded computer.

And Quinn...he was looking at her in horror, as if he couldn't believe what he'd done and with whom.

"Jesus," he muttered, dropping his hands from her. "I'm sorry. I shouldn't have done that."

She struggled to steady her breathing. Hard to do when her entire body still felt winded from that explosive kiss. "Then why did you?" she whispered.

He went silent, his brows drawn together in a frown. But instead of answering the question, he simply cleared his throat and said, "I can't let you go back to Autumn alone. You could be in danger. You need to be home, where your father can protect you."

"My father only wants to protect himself." She rubbed her temples in frustration. "He had me committed, even after I told him I didn't drive my car off a bridge."

Quinn didn't respond, simply frowned.

"I need to find the truth," she murmured. "I've been trying to figure out what happened to Layla for ten years. I can't stop now."

"Layla is dead," Quinn said emphatically.

"Yeah, and someone tried to kill me after her body was found." Tears pricked her eyelids. "When she disappeared, I knew she was dead. And I was right."

"Yes, you were. So why can't you let it go now?" He suddenly groaned. "Forget it. I know why you can't. Because you're Morgan Kerr."

She shot him a faint smile. "That's me, always the troublemaker..."

Quinn didn't return the smile. "Please, Morgan, let me take you home."

"No."

He let out a sigh, but before he could open his mouth to object, she hurried on. "Look, I know you don't owe me any favors. If anything, I'm the one who ought to be making amends." Her voice wavered. "But please, Quinn, do me this favor. Come back to Autumn with me."

He muttered a hasty expletive. "I already said no."

"And I'm trying to change your mind. I think the smartest move would be having you with me." She forced herself not to think about that crazy kiss or their turbulent history as she continued. "You're a mercenary. You could keep me safe, and since we both agree there was foul play out on that bridge, then my safety is definitely an issue."

He stayed silent. A gust of icy wind swept through the woods, lifting Quinn's dark hair, and Morgan noticed the blood on his temple had dried. She was tempted to reach out and touch the wound, but kept her hands to her side. She could clean the cut later. *After* he agreed to come with her. Which he would. She could see the resolve in his eyes crumbling.

She decided to give him one last push.

"You once told me you'd always protect me." She tilted her head. "What if I go alone and get hurt? Could you live with that, knowing I'd asked for your protection and you denied me?"

He gave a short bark of a laugh. "That's low, sweetheart, even for you."

She shrugged. "Did it work?"

Quinn released a heavy sigh. "What the hell do you think?"

Of all the stupid, moronic, asinine things Quinn had ever done in his thirty-two years of life, this one took the prize. What was he *thinking,* agreeing to take Morgan to Autumn? During the entire hike back to the main road, where he'd left his car, he'd been asking himself that question. And now, as he unlocked the doors of the black SUV, the answer still eluded him.

The best he could come up with? That flowerpot to the head had knocked a few screws loose.

"Thank you for doing this," Morgan said as she slid into the passenger seat.

He started the engine, then turned on the heat full-blast, hoping it might thaw the useless block of ice his brain had become. He couldn't do this. Just being near this woman was pure torture. He was *aching* for her, angry at her, torn between pulling her into his arms and pushing her far, far away.

Setting his jaw, he spared her a glance and said, "Buckle your seat belt."

He was about to move the gearshift when she reached out to stop him. Her hand was cold, but feeling her slender fingers on his hand sent a shot of pure heat to his groin. Unable to stop himself, he thought about the kiss they'd shared in the woods.

Again, what was he *thinking?* Kissing her had been foolish on so many levels. It had been wrong, and pointless, and... unbelievable. The second their lips met, he was transported back in time. The jolt of arousal, the sense of belonging, the sheer *rightness* of having Morgan's mouth pressed against his own. It was almost as if they'd never parted.

He abruptly shrugged off her hand, angry at his train of thought. No matter how mind-blowing that kiss had been, it didn't change a damn thing. He and Morgan *had* parted. She'd cast aside the man she supposedly loved so her dear old daddy's reputation wouldn't be tainted.

"Let me clean you up first," she said softly, completely oblivious to the turmoil riddling his body.

"I'm fine," he said gruffly.

"Humor me."

Gritting his teeth, he watched as she rummaged around in her purse, finally pulling out a small pack of tissues and a travel tube of hand sanitizer. "This will do the trick," she said with a nod. She squirted some hand sanitizer on a tissue. "Lean forward."

He didn't move. No way was he leaning closer to her. Last time he got too close, he'd ended up with his tongue down her throat.

Morgan rolled her blue eyes. "Why is it that when it comes to injuries, men are either big babies or irritating tough guys?" Without waiting for an answer, she slid toward him and swiftly pressed the tissue to his temple.

He flinched, ignoring the tiny sting of pain, and patiently sat there as she wiped up the dried blood on his cheek. When her scent wafted up to his nose, that intoxicating dose of flowers, honey and woman, he held his breath, determined not to let it affect him. Damn it, she was too close. Way too close, and... why was she running her fingers through his hair?

He hissed out a breath, and her hand froze. "You have... ceramic in your hair," she said, her husky voice coming out shaky.

Quinn curled his fingers around her slender wrist and moved her arm away. "I can do it," he muttered. Avoiding her eyes, he raked the tiny shards from his hair, then repeated his earlier request. "Will you buckle up now?"

When she was strapped in, he shifted gears, drove off the gravel shoulder and pulled onto the dark two-lane road.

"So...I guess I should call my father," Morgan said. "Do you have a cell phone?"

His voice came out brusque. "There's no service out here. We'll call him when we get closer to civilization."

That was one call Quinn wasn't looking forward to. No doubt the senator would be furious when he found out where they were headed, nor would he be pleased that Quinn had decided to stick around and help her.

"Tony will be worried, too," Morgan said absently. "Remind me to call him after I speak to Dad."

"How's your brother these days?" Quinn found himself asking. He'd always been fond of Morgan's older brother. The guy had a lust for life, a perpetual lopsided grin and a contagious live-in-the-moment attitude that Quinn had always found oddly refreshing.

"He's doing well," Morgan replied, smiling. "He's happily working at that advertising firm. And he actually has a girlfriend. Finally got over his commitment issues."

Ah, commitment issues. Quinn knew all about those. In fact, when he'd first met Morgan, the last thing he wanted to do was enter into a relationship with her. For a former foster kid who'd pretty much been abandoned by everyone he'd ever cared about, getting close to someone had been as appealing as having his legs waxed.

Yet Morgan managed to break down his walls. Snaked her way right into his heart, until he'd actually started to believe happily ever after didn't just exist in fairy tales.

Evidently he should've stuck to his original viewpoint.

"I think the first item on our agenda should be talking to the medical examiner," Morgan said, snapping him from his thoughts. "I was in town the day Layla's body was found, but the M.E. couldn't meet with me until the next morning. Unfortunately, my car wound up in the river that night, so I never made it to the meeting."

"Were Layla's remains buried or cremated?"

"Neither. The M.E. still needed to properly examine them, so we held a memorial service at the church. There might be a burial in a few weeks, if Layla's parents feel up to it."

"You need to be careful about who you speak to," Quinn warned. "We still don't know who tried to kill you, but there's a high probability that someone from town caused the accident."

She swallowed. "What if they try again?"

He could feel those beautiful blue eyes on him, and when he turned, he saw the anxiety in them. It was almost the exact same expression she wore the week before their wedding, when she'd asked him if he minded postponing it until after her father's reelection campaign.

He'd minded, all right. Minded so much he'd dropped an ultimatum in her lap, one she promptly tossed right back at him.

"Quinn?" she prompted.

He knew she wanted reassurance, a promise, a guarantee that he would stick by her side during this potentially dangerous investigation.

He was tempted to tell her to go to hell.

But when he opened his mouth, what came out was, "As long as you're with me, you won't get hurt, Morgan."

Too bad he couldn't say the same for himself.

Chapter 4

They were about forty minutes from the town of Autumn when Quinn pulled in to the parking lot of a twenty-four-hour gas station. He didn't need gas. Nature wasn't calling, either. But the past half hour, which involved long silences broken by Morgan's tentative attempts at making conversation, had finally gotten to him.

Parking in front of the small, well-lit building, he shut off the engine and grabbed his cell phone from the cup holder he'd shoved it into.

"Are we calling my father?" Morgan asked, that husky voice tinged with—shockingly enough—bitterness.

Well, it was about damn time he heard that tone in relation to the senator. God knew he'd felt that same spark of bitterness hundreds of times over the years. Yet he'd tried to be decent about it, hadn't revealed precisely how much he loathed the man who'd sired her, all the while wondering how Morgan could be so blind to Senator Kerr's machinations, why she constantly defended the bastard.

Her father's constant interference in their lives had been annoying, to say the least. If Quinn made dinner reservations for the three of them, Edward canceled them, forcing them to dine wherever he chose. For Morgan's birthday, they'd planned a trip to Fiji—only to abandon their plans so Morgan could attend some fancy-pants dinner her father insisted she go to. Quinn, of course, wasn't on the guest list. Morgan's father tried hard to keep Quinn's association with his daughter under wraps. Apparently a soldier for hire wasn't good enough for a daughter Senator Kerr didn't even truly care about.

Quinn had put up with it all, while Morgan remained unaware of his feelings toward her father. But then came the proverbial straw that broke the camel's back—the senator's insistence that they postpone the wedding. Quinn hadn't held back after that, and all the malicious—and well-deserved—thoughts he'd ever had about Morgan's father spilled out during that last confrontation.

"*I'm* making the call," he corrected. She opened her mouth to object but he held up a hand. "Don't argue with me on this. We both know how easily you give in to the man. If you want to go to Autumn, I make the call."

Without letting her respond, he pulled the door handle and stepped out of the SUV. The late night air immediately chilled him, but he welcomed the cool rush. Anytime he was around Morgan he was liable to get hot. Uncomfortably so.

Pausing near a trash can overflowing with coffee cups and dirty wrappers, he punched in the number for the senator's private line.

"Did you find her?" came the brisk answer.

As always, he stifled the urge to spit out a nasty reply. "Yes," he said.

"Thank God. I knew you would. Are you on your way back to the city?" The relief in the senator's voice was unmistakable. No doubt Kerr considered this another successful triumph.

Tuck Morgan back in the psych ward before she could stir up trouble for dear old dad.

Quinn wished he could see the man's face when he dropped the next bomb on him, but he could live with hearing the outrage.

"Actually..." He grinned. Couldn't stop it, couldn't help it. He'd dreamed of sticking it to the senator for years. "I'm not bringing her back."

Deafening silence.

Followed by a foul curse, then, "*What?* Why the *hell* not?"

"She doesn't want to come home," he said simply. "And I don't feel inclined to take her."

"You son of a bitch. That wasn't our deal."

"We didn't make a deal. I told you I'd find her, and I did. I never said I would bring her back."

He'd planned on it, though. When he found her in the cabin, he had every intention of driving her right back to D.C. and depositing her on Edward's doorstep. But that was before she told him what really happened on the bridge. No matter how badly he wanted—no, *needed*—to be away from her, he couldn't abandon her if she was in danger. If he left, who would protect her?

"I swear to God, Quinn, if you don't get in the car and drive her back to the hospital where she belongs, I'm going to sic every cop in the city on you."

"Let me guess, you'll charge me with kidnapping? Yeah, I expected that threat." Quinn's grin widened. "You won't do it, though."

"I sure as hell will."

"No," he answered coolly. "You won't. Because if you do, I'm going to unleash a media storm on you. I'll contact the press, tell them all about how you fabricated Morgan's mental illness in order to keep her in line. I won't stop there, either. If it strikes my fancy, maybe I'll spin a few tales of my own, lob a few accusations your way, like, shoot, I don't know, illegal campaign funds? Bribery? That'll get them salivating."

Senator Kerr sounded absolutely livid. "I have done nothing of the sort."

"Yeah, but the media doesn't know that, do they? Either way there'll be a few black spots on your name, no matter what the truth is."

The line went quiet for a moment. "Why are you doing this?" Kerr finally asked, sounding wary.

"Because someone tried to kill your daughter last week," Quinn retorted stiffly. "And unlike you, that actually concerns me."

"Nobody tried to kill her," Kerr said in frustration. "She was hallucinating—"

"Save the lies for someone else. I don't give a damn if you believe her or not. I'm just letting you know the reason I've agreed to help her. And I'm also giving you a friendly reminder that if you attempt to have me arrested, the results won't be pretty."

"You're a ruthless bastard, Adam."

"Takes one to know one, doesn't it, Edward?" he said glibly. "Now, if you'll excuse me, Morgan and I have somewhere we need to be."

The senator hung up.

A rush of exhilaration swept up Quinn's spine. Oh, yeah. A long time coming, that's what this confrontation was. And he knew his threat wouldn't go unheeded. The senator would not call the police. He'd stew about this latest development in private, of course, but risk a possible scandal? Never.

Closing the phone, Quinn headed back to the car, only to pause midstep. A wave of uneasiness washed over him as he spotted Morgan leaning against the back of the SUV, her expression a combination of anger and respect.

"You heard all that?" he asked.

She nodded.

"Well, let's have it then." Disgust rose up his throat. "I antagonized your poor, innocent father, right? Overstepped my boundaries?" When she didn't take the bait, he lifted a sardonic brow. "Huh. Where's that famous Kerr temper?"

Morgan ran a hand through her silky hair. "I'm not going to tear into you. You did good."

Though it was rare, Quinn was stunned speechless.

"I can only imagine what he was saying to you," she added, shaking her head in irritation. "He wants me back in the psych ward, right? Well, I won't go back. And if keeping me out of there meant you had to launch a few threats in his direction, I can't fault you for that."

Again with the bitterness. A part of him wanted to lash out at her, too, demand to know why she was only now opening her eyes to her father's true colors. Why not two years ago, when it had actually mattered? But he held his tongue. Somewhat. Still, he had to ask, "Where is this coming from?"

Morgan met his inquisitive gaze head-on. "He didn't believe me," she said simply, then turned on her heel and headed back to the passenger side.

Quinn had stood up for her. Although it hardly meant he'd forgiven her, and it definitely didn't mean he'd welcome her back into his life with open arms, Morgan couldn't fight the small thrill that shot through her body. Her father had the annoying ability to bulldoze any man who came into her life, but not Quinn. He'd *threatened* a senator. Her father. For *her*.

Morgan buckled up her seat belt and watched from the corner of her eye as Quinn started the engine. God, she wanted to throw her arms around him. She wanted to thank him again for what he'd done just now, for that unshakable belief he still seemed to have in her, despite the messy way they'd ended things.

The memory of their breakup struck a chord of regret. No,

she didn't want to think about that heartbreaking goodbye. Right now, as she sat next to the man who'd just defended her to her father, she couldn't stop thinking about the *hello*.

"Do you remember the day we met?" she burst out, unable to stop the words from leaving her mouth.

Quinn's head jerked in her direction, surprise etched in his rugged features. Surprise that soon dissolved into wariness. "Of course I remember," he said gruffly.

But along with the wariness, there was tenderness in his voice. Tender. When they'd first met she would never have expected a man like Adam Quinn to possess even an ounce of tenderness. He'd been all business that day, clad in camo pants and an olive-green T-shirt that clung to his sweat-soaked chest. He'd marched around that refugee camp, barking orders at his men—and at her.

"I thought you were such a jerk," she admitted with a grin. "You kept ordering me to get on the 'damn chopper.'"

"And you kept refusing," he replied mildly.

She shrugged and leaned back in her seat. "My story wasn't finished. And the threat didn't feel real."

But it had been real, hadn't it? Quinn's team was sent in to extract all the relief workers and journalists at the camp, after intel came in that a rebel group planned to raid it. Morgan held on to the end, though, leaving on the last chopper out of the Congo. Twelve hours later, the rebels had massacred half the camp.

"I wish we could have helped them," she whispered.

"We could only help ourselves."

Morgan swallowed, blocking the images of the carnage from her mind. She hadn't seen it firsthand, but she'd viewed the photos later, horrified by the deaths of all those innocent victims. And yet amidst chaos and disaster, she'd fallen in love with Quinn, the big, tough mercenary who for some reason had fallen for her, too.

"I don't know what you saw in me," she confessed, turning

to meet his dark green eyes. "I was a total mess. Dirty clothes, rumpled hair. But when we landed in D.C., you called me beautiful." Her throat tightened at the memory.

His hard gaze softened. "You *were* beautiful." He half grinned. "Not to mention stubborn, irritating, demanding…you wouldn't quit until you got me to agree to an interview."

"Which you didn't end up doing," she reminded him.

No, they never got around to that interview. Drinks at his hotel led to dinner, which led to a nightcap, which led to a night of spontaneous lovemaking that left them both shocked and breathless. A one-night stand, that's what she thought it would end as, but two years later, they'd been engaged to be married.

"That first night," she continued, her voice coming out wobbly. "It was the best night of my life, did I ever tell you that?"

Their eyes locked again, and Morgan heard a hiss of attraction in the air. Before she could stop it, the memory of their first time shot to the front of her brain. Quinn's chest, rippled with hard sinewy muscles, pressed against her bare breasts. The delicious heaviness of his body covering hers, the feel of his arousal slowly sliding inside her body. Completion. That's what it felt like, the first time he entered her.

From the flash of lust and remembrance in his eyes, she knew he was thinking about it, too, how right it had felt. How perfectly they'd fit together.

God, she wanted him back. So badly that her lips ached with the need to tell him she loved him, she missed him, she couldn't live without him.

But just before she could open her mouth, the fire in his eyes died, replaced by ice. A muscle twitched in his powerful jaw, and she saw his hands tighten over the steering wheel.

"Don't go there," he finally said, the ice in his eyes freezing his tone as well. "We're not taking a trip down memory lane, Morgan. We're finding out who tried to kill you."

She released a shaky breath. "I know. I didn't mean to—"

"Oh, you meant it, all right." Quinn's hard gaze slid over her face. "Reminding me of the day we met isn't going to make me forget the day we said goodbye."

"I know. I—"

"Don't play games with me, Morgan. I'm not interested in rekindling our affair."

Hurt seized her insides. "Affair? I think the two years we spent together means we went far past the affair stage."

"Yeah, I thought so, too," he said harshly. He cocked his head. "But considering everything, I've rethought that. You made it quite clear in the end what your priorities were, and our *relationship* wasn't one of them."

"That's not true," she protested. "I never wanted to end it. I just—"

"We're not going there," he said again, silencing her with another deadly look. "What's done is done. We're not together anymore and I don't plan on changing that in the near or distant future."

Each word was like a bullet straight to the heart. Was it possible for words to cause such extreme physical pain? Evidently so. Morgan's entire body felt bruised, her chest raw, her insides twisted with intense agony that brought a wave of nausea. Cruel. When had he become so cruel? Her heart ached again as she realized she was probably the cause of this new personality defect of his. God, why had she ever chosen her father over Quinn?

In hindsight, she knew she'd let her father dictate a large part of her life with Quinn. Constantly caved in to his demands, all the while knowing she was doing the wrong thing. Why hadn't she acted differently?

Stand by your father. Help him when he asks. He doesn't like to ask for help.

That's why. Her mother's words, the plea she'd made before she died, that's why Morgan made the choices she had.

But that didn't make it any easier. She knew she'd hurt Quinn, but she hadn't imagined the extent of the pain she'd caused him.

"Thanks for making that clear," she finally said, her voice as stiff as her shoulders. "I'll refrain from bringing up the past, if it makes you so uncomfortable."

With that, the conversation came to a screeching halt. Morgan glued her gaze to the window, watching the scenery whiz by. Tall pine trees lined both sides of the road, along with the naked skeletons of the oaks that had shed their leaves for the winter. The abundance of trees told her they were nearing Autumn. She'd loved growing up there, at least when her mom had been alive. Their estate rested on the edge of a forest, and during the summers she and Tony enjoyed hiking and exploring the woods.

Layla came along on their hikes, too, though not often. Tony had the annoying habit of teasing Morgan's best friend mercilessly when they were growing up, so Layla avoided him whenever she could.

Layla. Just thinking about her friend brought another jolt of pain to Morgan's belly. Layla's bones had been found in that forest. Not near the Kerr estate, closer to the outskirts of town. Whoever killed her buried her in the woods. Left her there to rot.

Morgan's throat tightened. Her friend hadn't deserved to die like that.

"We're here," Quinn said, breaking the silence.

Yep, they sure were. Morgan glanced at the bright green sign with the words Welcome to Autumn, experiencing a knot of trepidation. It was a familiar feeling, one she suffered each time she came home over the past ten years. And after what happened on her last visit, her anxiety levels were at an all-time high.

Quinn slowed the SUV as they drove into Autumn. It was past one o'clock in the morning, and the town was dark, but even bathed in darkness, it held an unmistakable charm. Quaint shops and little brick buildings lined each side of Main Street, the sidewalks were cobblestone, and old-fashioned lampposts stood proudly along the street. An enormous yellow banner had been strung from two lampposts on opposite ends of the street, advertising the annual winter festival the town held each November.

Quinn glanced at the banner. "What exactly are sapsicles?" he asked warily.

She bit back a laugh. "Maple syrup Popsicles, snow cones, too. Old Mr. McMurty sells them at the festival every year."

He made a face. "Hope the town has a good dentist. I imagine the rate of sapsicle-related cavities is quite high."

"Still living sugar-free, I see," she said drily.

He raised a brow in her direction. "I'm thirty-two years old and cavity-free. Can you say the same?"

Morgan hid another smile, then grew annoyed with herself for even feeling the urge to show mirth after the way he'd spoken to her earlier. So what if Quinn still avoided sweets? So what if she'd teased him mercilessly about it in the past? This wasn't the past. As he'd so candidly told her, the past was over. And the future held nothing for them.

Tears stung her eyes. She quickly blinked, forcing the traitorous tears to retreat.

"Turn left at this stop sign coming up," she said, wincing at the hoarseness of her voice.

Fortunately, Quinn didn't seem to notice how close to breaking down she actually was. He followed her directions, turning left, then right, then following the dark asphalt road she indicated.

She'd never brought him home before. As they pulled onto the winding driveway leading to the Kerr estate, Morgan wondered how he would react to the house. When they were together, she was always careful not to talk too much about her wealth. Quinn had been carted from foster home to foster home growing up, and his less than luxurious upbringing often made her feel guilty.

A pair of enormous wrought-iron gates greeted them at the end of the drive. Since the gates were always locked tight and required a code on the keypad in order to part, Morgan's body stiffened when she found the gates gaping open.

"What the…" Her jaw hardened, her eyes suddenly focusing on the car parked on the circular driveway in front of the mansion.

Quinn drove through the open gates and shot her a wry look. "Can you honestly say you're surprised? Your father's a smart man—he knew precisely where you wanted to go."

"I still can't believe him." She met Quinn's gaze with a frown, then glanced back at the police cruiser sitting ominously on the smooth pavement.

Chapter 5

Sheriff Jake Wilkinson looked like a man ready for a fight as he stepped out of the cruiser and approached the SUV. Morgan unbuckled her seat belt, studying the man through the windshield, and, as usual, marveling at the fact that he looked exactly the same as he did in high school. Six feet tall, with a stocky chest and the arms of a bouncer, Jake had been the star linebacker on the high school football team, and his don't-mess-with-me attitude had followed him to adulthood. Back then, he was always itching for a good fight, often throwing the first punch. According to some acquaintances in town, that hadn't changed much, only now he had a badge to go along with his fists.

Morgan was not a fan of Jake Wilkinson. Hadn't liked him back then, didn't like him now.

"The sheriff, I presume?" Quinn murmured.

"Yep," she murmured back. "My father must have called him the second you two got off the phone. You're right, he knew exactly where we would go."

Quinn paused for a moment. "Sheriff dated her, right?"

"Yep."

Quinn's eyes narrowed at the man approaching their vehicle. "Isn't the person closest to the victim usually the likeliest suspect?"

"Yep." Morgan sighed. "Come on, let's get this over with."

She and Quinn got out of the car. From the corner of her eye, she noticed Quinn had squared his shoulders, a sure sign he was geared up for a possible altercation. And if it came to one, she suspected Quinn could take the sheriff easily.

Jake's wide mouth was creased in a frown as she stepped closer to him. His dark-eyed gaze rested on her briefly before shifting to examine Quinn. The way he studied the other man, there might as well have been a neon sign with the words *testosterone overload* flashing across Jake's forehead.

She stifled a sigh. "Hello, Jake."

"Morgan." He gave a curt nod of greeting before turning to Quinn. "Adam Quinn, right?"

Quinn offered a nod of his own, along with a cheerless smile. "What can we do for you, Sheriff, at, oh—" he made a show of looking down at his watch "—one thirty-eight in the morning?"

Jake ran a hand through his jet-black hair before lowering it to the gun holstered at his hip. His fingers rested on the weapon ever so casually, yet the entire move screamed intimidation. "Your father informed me you were heading back to town," he said. "So I decided to come here and see how you're doing. You know, considering the last time you were here I was pulling your car out of the river."

Morgan bristled at his words. The night she went over the bridge, she'd told Jake about the other car. Like her father, he hadn't believed her.

"I'm fully recovered, thank you," she returned stiffly.

"Uh-huh." The tone of his voice revealed precisely what he thought of the matter—suicidal chick in denial.

"Let me guess," she said. "You've made no headway in tracking down the car that was behind me that night."

Jake's obsidian eyes flashed. "I investigated your claim and found nothing to indicate there had been another car on the bridge."

"Of course." Each word dripped with sarcasm.

The sheriff ignored her tone. "How long are you planning on staying?" His gaze shifted from her to Quinn, distrustful.

"Does it matter?" Quinn asked with insincere friendliness. "This is where Morgan grew up." He gestured to the massive house behind them. "Her family still owns this house. She's allowed to be here as long as she wants, no?"

"Sure, as long as she doesn't decide to interfere with my investigation."

Anger skimmed up Morgan's spine. "The investigation into Layla's death, you mean? The one that poses a serious conflict of interest for you, seeing as you dated Layla?"

Jake's fingers tightened over the butt of his gun. "Layla and I broke up before she disappeared and you know it, Morgan."

"That doesn't mean you didn't kill her," she answered sweetly.

She opened her mouth to say more, but Quinn's hand suddenly dug into her waist. He palmed her hip hard, sending the clear message to cool it. Despite the warning in his touch, she welcomed it. The feel of his long, warm fingers sent a sizzling rush through the material of her sweater and burned her skin.

Ignoring the intense reaction, she focused on the sheriff, whose hard gaze didn't waver. "I'm a journalist, Jake," she said, softening her tone. "And Layla was my best friend. I have every reason to want to find out what happened to her."

"Finding that out is the police's job. *My* job," he clarified.

"Do you have any leads?" she asked.

His jaw twitched. "No."

"Suspects?"

"No, but—"

She hurried on. "Then what's the harm in another pair of eyes, another brain trying to solve this puzzle?"

Irritation flashed in his eyes. "I'm warning you, Morgan, don't stick your nose in my investigation."

She disregarded the threat and said, "I want access to the crime scene and Layla's remains."

"No way," Jake said flatly. He made a frustrated sound. "Your father told me you'd try to interfere. Well, I'm making it clear right here and now, if you mess around with my case, I'm charging you with obstruction."

Morgan swallowed back her anger. Antagonizing Jake wouldn't help the situation, but she was unbelievably tempted to lash out. Instead, she drew in a calming breath. "I'm a good journalist. I could help—"

"You're mentally unstable," Jake interrupted, his voice colder than a glacier. "I read the newspapers, I know about the delusions, the reckless behavior."

The fury she'd swallowed down rushed up her throat and scorched her cheeks. "I am *not*—"

The fingers at her hip dug in deeper. Quinn, who'd been silent up until now, cut her off quickly. "Fine, Sheriff, we hear you loud and clear."

Jake's suspicious gaze shifted to the other man.

"Neither Morgan nor I will interfere with the investigation," Quinn went on. His tone was composed and friendly, but the hard set of his broad shoulders revealed he wasn't pleased with this turn of events, either. "I brought Morgan here so she could recover from the accident away from the media in D.C. We plan on keeping a low profile anyway."

Some of the suspicion in the sheriff's gaze dimmed. "Good," he finally said, nodding. "Stay out of my way, and we won't have any problems." He lifted his hand from his holster. "You two have a good night."

Gritting her teeth, Morgan watched as Jake walked back to his cruiser, opened the door and slid inside. A moment later, the engine roared to life and then he was gone.

After the cruiser disappeared through the gates, Morgan brushed Quinn's hand off her waist and spun to face him. "I have *every* intention of investigating my best friend's murder."

A fleeting expression of amusement crossed his face. "Of course. Who said you couldn't?"

"You. You just told Jake—"

"I lied. You honestly think I'd bring you back here only to make you sit at home twiddling your thumbs?"

Relief shimmied up her spine. Then she faltered. "But he won't let us see the crime scene. And I'm pretty sure he's going to order everyone involved in the case not to talk to us, including the coroner, which means we won't get access to her remains."

A spark of humor lit his green eyes. "Have you forgotten what I do for a living, sweetheart? I'm a mercenary. We live and breathe *covert*. Don't worry, you'll have access to anything you want."

Although she should've still been furious at him for the way he'd spoken to her earlier, Morgan's anger thawed, replaced by a warm rush that surrounded her heart. Licking her dry lips, she tilted her head to meet his eyes and said, "Thank you."

The conversation with that ass of a sheriff had made it difficult to examine his surroundings, but with the distraction gone, Quinn was finally able to really look around, and what he saw floored him. He knew Morgan's family was wealthy, but this house…hell, house? Calling it a house was like calling Andre the Giant a dwarf.

Three stories high, the French colonial-style mansion resembled the White House, with enormous limestone pillars flanking the entrance, wide marble steps leading to a pair of intricately carved front doors, and large balconies with wrought-iron railings on the second and third floors.

Morgan unlocked the door and beckoned for him to follow her into the front foyer. White marble spanned the enormous space, making Quinn feel as if he was committing a grievous sin as his big black boots connected with the pristine floor. Morgan seemed oblivious to his turmoil as she stepped forward in her sneakers, leaving a trail of mud on her way to the light switch. She flicked the switch, and the foyer lit up, revealing a crystal chandelier that belonged in Buckingham Palace, and two spiral staircases leading to the second and third floors.

"Don't worry about getting the floor dirty," Morgan said when she noticed him hesitating. "I'll mop it up in the morning."

He took a tentative step, his gaze drifting to a shadowy room to the right, which seemed to boast not one, but *two* shiny black grand pianos.

"The music room," Morgan supplied, following his gaze.

He finally found his voice. "I didn't realize anyone in your family was musical."

"We're not." She rolled her eyes. "But as my father says, every home needs a music room."

Quinn fought the urge to mention that said music room was the size of his apartment. Hell, the foyer alone was bigger than most people's homes.

He wasn't surprised that Morgan had never brought him back here before. Knowing her, she'd be embarrassed by the gaudy show of wealth. And the fact that her father spent most weekends here was probably another reason she hadn't invited him. Not that he minded—he'd rather cut off his own arm than spend his free time with Senator Kerr.

"Would you like a tour?" Morgan asked. "Or would you rather go straight to bed?"

Quinn's mouth turned to cotton. Damn, this woman was not allowed to say the word *bed*. Even after an escape from the psych ward, a run through the woods and a two-hour car ride, she still looked as beautiful as ever. Blond strands had fallen loose from her ponytail, framing her heart-shaped face like ribbons of gold, and her cheeks were flushed from the cold, or perhaps from their encounter with Wilkinson. Either way, the rosy blush made her look unbelievably sexy.

When his groin tightened, Quinn forced himself to remember what he'd told her in the car. He was not here to rekindle their romance. He wouldn't let himself.

"A quick tour would be okay," he said gruffly, deciding it was probably best to stall going into a bedroom with Morgan for as long as possible.

"Quick isn't going to be feasible. Did you see the size of this house?" She gave a rueful smile. "All right, let's see what I can do."

Quinn didn't say much as she took him around the first floor, showing him the famous music room, two living rooms and a sitting room—"I'm not sure what the difference is," she'd admitted—a kitchen boasting so much black marble and stainless steel his eyes hurt, two studies and a library that apparently contained over five thousand books.

"Ready for the second floor?" Morgan made a show of glancing at a watch she didn't wear. "We've got another hour or two."

He started to follow her back to the foyer, then halted. The hall they were in was lined with portraits, and one in particular caught his eye. In a beautiful gilded frame, a portrait of a stunning blonde with enormous blue eyes, delicate features and a long regal neck.

"My mother," came Morgan's soft voice.

He knew who it was before she even spoke; he'd seen pictures of her mother before. Besides, there was no mistaking the resemblance. Only, Patricia Kerr looked far more fragile than the daughter she'd given birth to. The eyes were too soft, the mouth too tender. She lacked the sparkle of humor, the fire, the glint of stubbornness, qualities her daughter possessed in spades.

"She was very…fragile," Morgan confessed, using the exact adjective that had entered his mind.

Quinn gave her a sideways glance and saw the sorrow swimming in her eyes.

"She hated conflict," Morgan went on. "Arguments made her nauseous, and she was so sensitive. If someone in town said an unkind word to her, she would stay in her room for days, inconsolable."

"She sounds…" His voice drifted. The word he wanted to use was *weak* but he couldn't bring himself to say it, not when Morgan's face shone with such obvious love for her mother.

But Morgan knew him well. "Weak?" she suggested. "I guess in a sense, she was." Her features softened, and suddenly she looked very much like the woman in the portrait. "But she was also very sweet. She loved me, and she adored Tony. Unlike my father, she spent a lot of time with us when we were kids. She was a good mother, Quinn."

"I don't doubt that." He cleared his throat. "Come on, let's head upstairs."

The second-floor tour ended up being quick. Each member of the house had their own wing, decorated in a way that distinctly revealed the personality of the person it belonged to. The senator's wing was done in shades of gold and black. Pale creams and yellows filled Patricia Kerr's rooms. Tony's wing was blue and green, with a splash of yellow thrown in here and there. And Morgan's wing…

"Pink?" he said, raising his eyebrows.

Morgan paused at the doorway of her childhood bedroom, making a face at the pale pink walls. "My parents chose it. I think they believed they could tame my wild and tenacious streak if they suffocated me with ladylike colors." She glanced at him and shrugged. "I would've chosen red."

Quinn couldn't help a grin. "Of course you would."

Morgan shut the door, then took him up to the next level, quickly showing him the playrooms she and Tony had used as children, another study and half a dozen guest rooms.

"You can sleep here." She flicked on the light to reveal a room with navy blue walls and gray trim, a queen-size bed with a deep gray bedspread and shimmery blue curtains over a large bay window that overlooked the backyard.

"Is the room okay?" she asked.

"It's fine."

"Thanks again for handling Jake. I was perilously close to losing my temper when you stepped in."

He smiled faintly. "No problem. Though I'm not sure it was a good idea letting him know you've considered the notion that he might have killed Layla."

She sighed. "I know. I couldn't help it. Jake has always rubbed me the wrong way."

"I can see why. The guy is a first-class jerk." Quinn headed for the bed and sank down on the edge, then bent down to unlace his boots. As he removed the mud-caked footwear, he glanced at Morgan. "Do you think he did it?"

"Honestly? I don't know. Is he capable of it? I think so." She leaned against the doorway. "He always had a temper, used to pick fights with any guy who looked at Layla."

Quinn kicked aside his boots. "Did she break up with him, or was it the other way around?"

"She broke things off. And I know for a fact Jake didn't take the breakup well, which is why—" Morgan paused midsentence, a flush sweeping across her cheeks.

It took a second for him to figure out the reason for the

blush. In the midst of their conversation, he'd started to remove his shirt. His hands froze on the hem of the sweater, then shoved the material back down to his waist. Damn it. It irked the hell out of him to realize he'd fallen right back into old habits. He used to undress in front of Morgan back when they lived together. She'd be filling him in about the latest developments in a story she was working on, he'd be removing his clothing, and…well, there wouldn't be much talking after that.

She betrayed you.

All it took was that one little reminder. Quinn stood abruptly, pushing away the unwelcome memories. He'd meant what he told her in the car. He wasn't interested in revisiting the past.

"It's late," he said coolly. "We'll finish this discussion in the morning, and figure out our next move."

He might as well have said "get out," yet Morgan lingered in the doorway, a hesitant flicker in her gorgeous blue eyes. Her bottom lip trembled, mouth parted slightly, as if she wanted to say something. After a moment, her shoulders sagged, and the expression in her gaze dissolved into resignation.

"You're right. We'll talk in the morning. Good night, Quinn."

"Good night, Morgan."

He watched her go, then walked to the door and closed it. He was tempted to lock it, too, add another barrier between him and Morgan, but he knew a locked door wasn't going to quell the traitorous rush of desire coursing through his body. Since the second he'd laid eyes on her in that cabin, after two years of trying to push her out of his head, he'd wanted her. Wanted her so badly it shocked him that he'd been able to hide it for this long.

Well, he wasn't hiding it any longer, was he? He shot a rueful glance at his groin, which was harder than ever and bitterly reprimanding him for the discomfort he'd put it through all night.

She betrayed you, he reminded himself—and his body.

Keeping those three words in the forefront of his brain, he undressed with a sigh and slid into bed.

Chapter 6

Quinn awoke the next morning to the brutally frigid breeze coming in from the window he'd left open. Sometime during the night he'd kicked the covers off. They now lay at the foot of the bed in a crumpled heap, while his entire body felt like it had been stuffed in a freezer. The glaring red numerals of the clock on the nightstand informed him it was eight o'clock, which meant he'd only gotten five hours of sleep. Oh, well. He'd functioned on less sleep before. On his last assignment he'd stayed awake for days.

Sighing, he swung his legs over the side of the bed, wincing when his ice-cold feet connected with the ice-cold parquet floor. Ignoring the goose bumps on his bare chest, he reached for the clothes he'd worn yesterday and put them on. Fortunately, he had some gear in the trunk of his car. Always be prepared, wasn't that the Boy Scouts' motto?

He smiled wryly to himself. As if he would know. He'd spent his childhood defending himself from abusive foster fathers and wondering when his next meal would be, not learning to tie knots and eating s'mores around a campfire with other boys.

Leaving the guest room, he went downstairs. The house was dark and quiet, and yet again he shook his head as he reached the front foyer. He'd never been surrounded by such extravagant wealth. It was slightly disconcerting.

When he stepped outside, the cold late-October air hit him like a fist to the gut, chilling the tips of his ears and burning his lungs when he inhaled it. With brisk strides he headed for the car, grabbed his duffel from the trunk and went back inside. Upstairs, he walked into the bathroom adjoining his room, where smooth black marble and a Jacuzzi tub greeted him. After a quick shower, he dressed in a pair of jeans, a blue button-down over a long-sleeved wool shirt and his trademark boots.

As he tied his laces, he heard pipes creaking from below, followed by the distant sound of water. He forced himself not to picture Morgan in the shower, and failed miserably. It was far too easy to imagine her standing under the hot spray as water sluiced down her sleek, curvy body.

To distract himself, he pulled out his cell phone and checked his messages. One from a contact at the CIA, though he had no intention of taking another assignment from the agency for a long while, not after all the red tape he'd had to wade through the last time. Two messages from Murphy, his fellow merc and right-hand man.

He called Murphy back without listening to the messages, and was greeted with a brisk hello. Darius Murphy was former navy, all business all the time, and the most efficient soldier Quinn had ever encountered.

"Hey, Murph, what's going on?" he asked, balancing the cell between his ear and shoulder as he bent down to make the bed. An old army habit—he couldn't leave a room without making the damn bed.

"Got a call from the CEO of a pharmaceutical company,"

Murphy answered. "Guy's daughter was kidnapped by some nasty dudes in Caracas. Apparently they're pissed off at Mr. CEO for testing his latest vaccines on some of the villagers there."

Quinn tucked the sheets into the edge of the bed frame, then smoothed out the duvet. "He wants us to extract the girl?"

"Yes, sir." After five years of working together, Murphy still referred to him as "sir," no matter how many times Quinn told him to cut it out.

"Think you and the guys can handle it on your own?"

"Yes, sir."

He bent down to retrieve the throw pillows he'd tossed on the floor last night, fluffed them out and set them back on the bed. "I'm still held up here, so I can't fly out. I'll be a few more days probably, but I suspect our CEO won't wait that long, huh?"

"No, sir."

"Then do the extraction."

Rather than another "yes, sir," he got a long silence.

"Murph, you still there?"

"Yes, sir, still here." Another pause. "How's Morgan?"

Quinn stifled a sigh. He'd wondered when the other man would bring it up. "She's good, considering someone tried to kill her."

"Have you caught the son of a bitch?"

The vehemence in Murphy's tone didn't surprise him. Murph had always been Morgan's number-one fan. For the past two years he'd constantly harassed Quinn to forgive her, to stop being a stubborn ass and take her back.

But stubbornness had nothing to do with it. He'd had a damn good reason to walk away from Morgan, one Murphy would never understand. The guy had a wife who adored him, who waited patiently at home while her husband flew to some of the world's most dangerous hot zones and risked his neck time and time again. Elena Murphy's entire life revolved around her husband, and if she ever had to choose between him and someone else, there would be no contest.

Morgan, on the other hand, had made the wrong choice.

"Haven't caught him yet," Quinn answered. "But I will."

"And then?"

"And then I meet up with you guys and prepare for our next gig, whatever it may be."

"Sir…" Murphy's voice held a note of uncertainty. "Don't you want to stay longer, maybe patch things up?"

"There's nothing to patch up," he said stiffly. His ears perked at the sound of footsteps out in the hallway. "Look, I've got to go. Keep me posted about the extraction."

"Yes, sir." A beat of hesitation. "Say hi to Morgan for me."

Quinn disconnected the call just as a soft knock sounded at his door. "Come in," he barked.

The door swung open, and Morgan stepped into the room. She wore what he'd always considered her "senator's daughter" attire: a black silk blouse tucked into the waistband of sleek, green slacks, and black high heels that added two inches to her height. A spark of irritation lit his belly. Yes, she looked sophisticated, almost regal thanks to the elegant twist she'd tied her blond hair into, but he'd never liked seeing her in those types of outfits. She looked far more beautiful in a pair of faded jeans and a snug T-shirt.

She noticed him studying her wardrobe and shrugged. "I know. Stuffy as hell, huh? It's all I had in the closet." She rolled her eyes. "I didn't exactly have an overnight bag with me when I broke out of the psych ward." Before he could comment, she changed the subject. "So what's on the agenda for today? A visit to the woods where Layla's body was found?"

Quinn shook his head. "We'll save that for tonight."

Her sensual lips curved with amusement. "Right, I forgot.

You need the cover of darkness, being a man who walks in the shadows and all."

Despite himself, he smiled. "It's the only way I operate."

"Okay, so what should we do?"

"I figure we'll go into town, have some breakfast and listen to what the folks in town are saying about the fact that Layla's body was found. Maybe we'll overhear something worthwhile and get a lead." He tucked his cell phone in his pocket, adding, "Murphy says hi, by the way."

Morgan's perfect features softened, her gaze growing wistful. "How is he doing?"

"He's fine."

She smiled again, and the tiny dimple at her chin popped out. "Does he still call you 'sir'?"

"Yep."

She averted her eyes for a moment, studying the small oil landscape hanging on the wall opposite the bed. When she looked back at him, that wistfulness still floated around on her face like a restless feather. "I miss him. Tell him I said hello, okay?"

"I will."

A short silence fell. Morgan cleared her throat. "Uh, yeah, so maybe when we're in town we can pay a visit to the medical examiner, too. His name is Frank Davidson, and I'm hoping he'll let us see Layla's remains."

"Not if Jake Wilkinson has anything to say about it," Quinn replied drily. "I'm sure the good sheriff already ordered Davidson not to speak to you.

She shrugged. "Then we'll stop by Frank's office after our foray in the woods tonight." Mischief lit in her eyes. "Do you still have your lock-picking kit?"

Quinn shot her a stern look. "You know owning one of those is illegal, Morgan. I wouldn't dream of it."

A laugh—husky and melodic—slid out of her throat. "You, do something illegal? Perish the thought." She stepped toward the door, glanced back over her shoulder and added, "Good thing I have mine with me."

Another unwelcome grin tugged at his mouth. Fortunately Morgan's back was turned so she didn't witness the treacherous reaction. Damn it. He was so not allowed to enjoy being with her. They weren't lovers any longer. Hell, they weren't even friends. Obligation, that's the only reason he was here. She'd said so herself—he wouldn't be able to live with himself if something happened to her, especially if he could have prevented it. It wasn't because he still cared about her. Just duty and obligation. A favor to someone he'd once cared about, that's all.

Drawing in a steadying breath, he followed Morgan out the door.

Jessie's Restaurant was located in the heart of Autumn, across the street from the town square and the police station. It served the best breakfast in town, drawing in the crowds during the summer tourist season, and locals year-round. Morgan wasn't surprised to find the restaurant nearly filled to capacity when she and Quinn strode through the door.

She also wasn't surprised when most of the patrons swiveled their heads in her direction, then averted their gazes and whispered to one another. Last time she'd come home, she wound up in the bottom of the river. In a town that didn't see much excitement, her little swim had been big news, and evidently still was.

"Prepare to be gawked at for the next hour," she murmured to Quinn, who seemed completely unfazed by the unconcealed interest of Autumn's residents.

The restaurant consisted of diner-style booths against one wall, a long chrome counter on the other and tables scattered in the middle of the room. All the tables were occupied, but Morgan spotted an empty booth in the back. She and Quinn headed for it, while she tried valiantly to ignore the stares and whispers they encountered along the way.

She managed to smile at a few people, including Kelly Peters, a girl she'd gone to high school with, and Mark Hertz, the owner of the bowling alley. Neither smiled back, but Kelly did offer a small wave of greeting.

"I hate this," she hissed at Quinn as they slid into the booth. "They all think I drove off the bridge on purpose."

He seemed unperturbed. "So what? You know the truth, what does it matter what they think?"

With trembling hands, she shrugged out of her coat, then reached for the menu, wishing she could be as composed and unruffled as Quinn. It was a trait of his she'd always admired, his ability to let things slide, not let anything rile him up. Sure, he was intense, prickly at times, and definitely crabby when he was hungry, but in the two years they were together, she'd only seen him get angry—truly angry—once.

The day she'd asked to postpone their wedding.

"It bothers me," she answered, keeping her voice low. "I grew up with these people, went to school with them, hung out at their houses. And then..."

Then her mother died and everything changed. She'd been so upset, so lonely, and she'd dealt with the pain by acting out. Her father had always been demanding and controlling, but after her mom lost the battle with cancer, he grew worse. He'd decided to run for the senate then, constantly ordering Morgan to be good, to be prim and proper in public, keep up appearances. He never spoke to her other than to criticize, yet in public he played the part of the doting father, pretending they were the best of friends.

So she'd rebelled. Died her hair black, hung out with some of the wilder boys at school, stared smoking cigarettes with them in the woods behind Autumn High. And when her dad forgot her seventeenth birthday because he was too focused on his stupid campaign, she'd gone for that joyride with Cooper Hamm—after they stole his dad's pickup.

Her father had been livid. Sent her to a shrink. And a few days after that, he gave an interview saying his daughter was mentally troubled. He'd stuck to that story for ten years, singing the same song over and over again, until it got to the point that she almost started believing the lyrics.

And then she'd met Quinn, who made her realize she wasn't nuts, that her rebellious teenage years were just that— rebellious teenager years. When her father raised the issue again in his reelection campaign, with his passionate vow to help other parents with troubled children, she'd come to understand precisely what she was to her dad—a pawn. A campaign tool.

Yet because of the promise she'd made to her mother, she'd been forced to stick by her father's side.

And lost Quinn in the process.

Swallowing back the bitterness clinging to her throat, she pretended to study the menu. Breathe, she ordered herself. Ignore the stares. Forget the past.

She was repeating the mantra in her head when the waitress finally approached their booth. Morgan recognized her instantly. Beth Greenwood, another former classmate. A tall redhead with enormous breasts, Beth had been the head cheerleader and a first-class bitch. She'd married her high-school sweetheart—the star quarterback, of course— right after graduation, cranked out three children while still managing to maintain her sensational figure, and apparently cheated on her husband constantly, mostly with eligible tourists who drifted into town.

"Hello, Morgan," Beth said, the acid in her green eyes contradicting her sugar-sweet voice.

Morgan resisted a sigh. She and Beth had never gotten along. "Hey, Beth. How are the kids?"

Beth's fingers stiffened ever so slightly on her order pad. It was no secret she didn't pay much attention to her children.

"They're fine." Beth offered a big fake smile. "And you? Recovering from your…accident, I see."

Morgan bristled at the emphasis Beth placed on the word *accident*. "I'm doing great," she replied, pasting on a fake smile of her own.

Beth's catlike green eyes drifted in Quinn's direction. She studied him like a scavenger eyeing a juicy carcass. The blatant lust in her eyes brought a rush of annoyance and unwelcome jealousy to Morgan's gut. Beth Greenwood was a grade-A predator. It was a wonder her husband hadn't divorced her yet.

"I can see that," Beth drawled, her gaze never leaving Quinn's. "I assume this is the famous Adam Quinn?"

Quinn spared the drooling redhead a glance before turning back to his menu. "That would be me."

Beth's lips curved. "I can see why you never brought him here. Wanted to keep him all to yourself, didn't you, Morgan?"

Morgan set her jaw. "Can we order?"

Beth seemed unflustered by the sharp request. "Sure thing. What can I get for you?"

"Pancakes for me, and a cup of coffee, two sugars, no milk," Morgan said.

"I'll have the special," Quinn said. "And coffee, black."

Beth scribbled down their orders, then flounced off without another word. She had plenty to say at the counter, though. To Morgan's annoyance, Beth immediately began whispering with the other waitresses, all of whom turned to stare at Quinn with admiring eyes.

"Looks like you have a fan club," Morgan remarked, swallowing back the jealousy creeping up her throat.

Quinn leaned back against the vinyl seat, causing the material of his button-down to stretch across his broad chest.

Morgan's mouth instantly went dry as she stared at the defined ripples of his abdominal muscles, straining beneath his shirt. She'd never met anyone sexier than Quinn. No doubt about it, he was the stuff of fantasies.

Regret swarmed her body. He'd been more than a fantasy to her, her reality for two whole years. And like a fool, she'd blown it.

Maybe she truly was insane.

"Don't look so concerned," Quinn said, evidently believing her distress had something to do with the waitresses ogling him. "I'm not interested in the fan club or any of its members."

"No? Don't tell me nobody has sparked your interest these past two years." She injected a casual note to her voice, all the while dreading the answer.

His green eyes darkened. "If you're asking whether I'm dating anyone, then no. Relationships don't interest me any longer."

God, two years ago he'd been ready to marry her, and now he wasn't interested in even dating? The knowledge that she'd caused this change of heart made her chest ache with guilt and regret.

She opened her mouth to object, to tell him he shouldn't close himself off because of her, but he ended the discussion swiftly, asking, "How's work going?"

"Good." She made a self-deprecating face. "At least it was until last week. Patrick is probably going to fire me for going off the radar."

Patrick Garrison, her editor at *World at Large,* had done her a huge favor when he took a chance on her. He'd hired based on her writing, choosing to ignore her negative presence in the tabloids. All he demanded in return was hard work and that she keep a low profile. Fortunately, her stay in the psych ward hadn't made the papers, but she knew Patrick wouldn't be pleased that she hadn't checked in for several days.

"Speaking of Patrick, can I use your cell phone?" she asked Quinn. "I'm pretty sure my father took mine from my purse."

Quinn reached into his pocket, pulled out the phone and slid it across the table. "It's all yours."

Morgan keyed in the number for her voice mail, listened to the six messages she found there, and hung up with a sigh. "Yep, Patrick is not happy. Remind me to call him later."

Quinn nodded. "Sure thing. Now how about we do what we came here to do? Hear anything interesting?"

They spent the next ten minutes in silence, attempting to overhear the conversations in the restaurant. When Beth returned to the booth with their meals, the silence continued to drag as they ate and sipped their coffee. Fifteen minutes later, Morgan had learned that Mrs. Hertz, the florist, was in the hospital with a broken hip, Beth's husband had gotten drunk on Friday night and picked a fight with the sheriff and Margaret Hanson was pregnant again. Nothing about Layla. It was as if nobody in town gave a damn that Layla Simms's remains had been discovered last week. Then again, after ten years, Layla's disappearance probably wasn't on many people's minds anymore.

"Let's go," Quinn said the moment she set down her fork on her empty plate. "These people are either self-absorbed, or they simply don't care that one of their own was killed."

"I vote for self-absorbed," she murmured.

Quinn dropped a few bills on the table and stood up. He waited for her to slip into her black, knee-length pea coat, and then the two of them walked toward the exit. They reached the door just as a tall man with salt-and-pepper hair strode inside the restaurant. It was Jackson Hamm, the father of the boy she'd gone for the joyride with, and his wrinkled features hardened the moment he spotted her.

"Hi, Mr. Hamm," she said, offering a tentative smile.

The older man did not return the greeting. "Aren't you ashamed to show your face here, Ms. Kerr?"

The remark stung, but she forced herself to remain cordial. "I don't know what you mean."

"You've caused nothing but trouble for this town," Hamm replied with a frown. "You break the law, you seek attention, you embarrass not only your father but the rest of us. Do us all a favor, Ms. Kerr, and leave now before you cause more trouble."

From the corner of her eye, she saw Quinn's shoulders stiffen. Her own were pretty stiff, too, but again she attempted a polite smile. "I'm sorry you feel that way, Mr. Hamm. I can assure you, I didn't come here to cause trouble. I just wanted a quiet place to recover from the accident."

Hamm snorted. "Accident? Is that what you're calling it?" He shrugged out of his heavy wool coat and tucked it under his arm. "You're not fooling anyone. The entire world knows you attempted to take your own life. I don't know how Senator Kerr puts up with you."

Tears pricked at her eyelids. It took a serious amount of willpower to blink them back. She refused to cry in front of this resentful old man. "I'm sorry you feel that way," she said again, her voice trembling.

"Let's go," Quinn said curtly, not even acknowledging the other man's presence.

"And stay away from my son while you're here," Jackson Hamm barked at their retreating backs.

The second Morgan stepped out onto the sidewalk, two fat tears slid down her cheeks. She viciously swiped at them with the sleeve of her coat, keeping her back to Quinn so he wouldn't witness the show of weakness. Damn it. Damn them. Damn everyone in this town. The only reason she'd come back here over the past ten years was for her best friend, to preserve Layla's memory and discover the truth of her disappearance.

She hadn't come back for any of them, and she refused to let their hurtful words and curious eyes and smirks get to her.

"You okay?" Quinn asked quietly.

She wiped away the last tear before turning to face him. "I'm fine," she said. "He just blames me because his son Cooper and I took his car for a joyride ten years ago." She suddenly smiled, a humorless curve of the lips. "I wonder if I should go back in there and tell him it had been his son's idea."

"Don't exert any energy on that old bastard." Quinn shook his head. "You know, it's times like these that I'm almost grateful for my own upbringing. Being tossed around all over New York City seems a slight step above living in a small town where everyone knows your business."

"And constantly judges you," she added with a sigh. Then she paused. "What do you think he meant when he said the whole world knows the truth? My dad said he was keeping the accident out of the papers."

Quinn's gaze slid beyond her, and a frown creased his lips. "Looks like he lied."

Wrinkling her brow, Morgan turned in the direction of Quinn's gaze. She froze when she noticed the bank of newspaper boxes on the sidewalk. One headline in particular caught her attention, and sent anger spiraling through her body until it knotted in her intestines like a pretzel.

Senator's Daughter Recovering from Suicide Attempt

Chapter 7

By the time they returned to the Kerr estate, Morgan's mood had sunk from bad to dismal. The article in the *Washington Post* had been a blow, and the visit to the medical examiner's office wasn't much better. Dr. Frank Davidson made it clear he would not allow her and Quinn to view Layla's remains. Under pressure, he admitted the sheriff had spoken to him, but he hadn't backed down, either.

She and Quinn drove home with no leads and low morale, but hopefully tonight would change that. They planned to visit the woods where Layla's body had been found, then the morgue, followed by a stop at Jake's office, since she was convinced he was hiding something. It was going to be a busy night.

But first she had to get through the rest of the day, which meant spending however many hours with Quinn and forcing herself not to bring up the past, discuss the future and, the hardest thing of all, resist the urge to kiss him.

When they walked through the front door, Morgan told

him to wait in the living room while she went into the study she used whenever she was home to retrieve the files she had on Layla's disappearance. The phone was ringing when she entered the study, and just when she thought her day couldn't possibly get any worse, it did.

"Hey, Tony," she said after the caller ID revealed her brother's cell phone number.

"Why are you in Autumn?" was his irritated response.

She sighed and sank into the large leather chair at the mahogany desk. "I'm sure Dad already filled you in. I'm here to figure out what happened to Layla, and to me the night on the bridge."

A short silence descended, then a frustrated curse. "Look, I know you truly believe someone ran you off that bridge," Tony finally said. "However, there was no evidence to indicate that scenario."

"It's not a *scenario*," she shot back. "It's what happened. There was another car behind me, Tony."

"I know you believe that," he said again. His normally lively voice softened to a regretful note. "But I think you imagined it, Mor."

"I did not ima—"

He hurried on. "You were upset, you weren't concentrating on driving. I was there, remember? I saw you at the pub, saw how upset you were after Layla's memorial. You had too much to drink, kiddo, and you weren't in the right state of mind."

"What state of mind was I in then, Tony?" Sarcasm freely dripped from her tone. "The suicidal kind? God, you really think I tried to kill myself?"

"I think you were upset," he reiterated. He grew silent again, and she could practically see him dragging his fingers through his sandy blond hair, something he did whenever he was frustrated. "Morgan, I also think maybe it's time to consider going on medication."

She nearly dropped the phone. "Medication? Are you kidding me?"

"Your behavior isn't normal." He spoke in a calm, condescending tone usually reserved for young children and extremely crazy people—apparently she was the latter. "You know I'm on your side when it comes to how controlling Dad can be, but he has a point about this. For years you've been acting out, blaming other people for your destructive actions. And then that incident with the drugs—"

"I have never used drugs in my life," she snapped. "I was at a nightclub with friends and the owner decided to make a quick buck by claiming I was snorting coke in the bathroom. It never happened, Tony. You said you believed me."

"I did. I mean, I do." He released a heavy breath that reverberated through the telephone line. "I don't know what to believe anymore. All I know is that my little sister wound up in the bottom of a river, and now she's trying to conduct an investigation she was strictly ordered not to look into. Leave Layla's death to the cops, Morgan."

"You'd like that, wouldn't you?" she said, cringing at the snide note in her voice. "You never liked Layla, and you don't give a damn who killed her."

"See? It's this kind of behavior I'm talking about. You lash out whenever you feel antagonized."

She drew in a calming breath. "No, I'm lashing out because everyone in my life is accusing me of being suicidal, delusional and insane."

Another soft obscenity. "Do I need to come out there, Morgan?"

"Don't bother. Quinn's here. He can keep me in line," she said bitterly.

"Yeah, and there's another development I don't quite approve of. Did you get back together with the guy?"

"No, we didn't get back together. He's just helping me out."

She couldn't stop her next stinging remark. "Unlike you and Dad, he actually believes I might be in danger."

"Oh, for God's sake, you're not in danger. I think you need to—" Tony paused midsentence then groaned. "Damn it. I have to go. I'm meeting Caroline for dinner and I'm already ten minutes late."

Despite her anger and frustration at her brother, the mention of his new girlfriend sparked her interest. Tony had never been in a relationship that lasted more than a few days, so this was quite extraordinary. "You're still with Caroline?" she asked.

"Yes, and she's going to be ticked off at my lack of punctuality."

"Don't worry, just tell her you were on the phone with your psycho, suicidal sister," she said sweetly.

"Not funny, Morgan. Look, I'll call you tomorrow and we'll finish this discussion. Just promise me right now you won't harass Jake Wilkinson and stick your nose in his investigation."

She hesitated. "Fine, I promise. Happy now?"

"Yep."

They said goodbye, and Morgan placed the cordless phone back in its cradle. She didn't feel the least bit guilty about lying to Tony, though really, she hadn't exactly lied. She had no intention of harassing Jake, or interfering in *his* investigation. She simply planned on launching her own one.

I don't know what to believe anymore.

Her older brother's frank words buzzed around in her brain like a swarm of bees, causing her to lean back in the chair and lift her knees up to her chest. She wrapped her arms around herself, pressing her cheek against one knee, and the tears she'd been fighting all day finally made an appearance.

Oh, God. Was Tony right? Was she truly unstable?

No. No, she couldn't be. She hadn't imagined those headlights behind her. Hadn't hallucinated the scrape of metal as the other car slammed into her rear bumper, the way the wooden rail on the bridge had snapped like a twig from the weight of her car. The horrifying sense of vertigo as the car soared over the edge and fell ten feet into the river below. Grace River wasn't the deepest body of water, but deep enough that her entire car had been submerged, that the frigid water poured in from the open window and soaked the simple black dress she'd worn to Layla's memorial.

She still remembered the bone-deep terror slicing through her body like a sharp knife, her desperate attempts to open the driver's door. God, she could have died. Would have died, if it weren't for Colin Kincaid, the deputy who stopped his car on the bridge to investigate the broken railing. Kincaid dove into the cold water and pulled her out of the car, hauling her to the muddy riverbank, where he warmed her with his jacket as they waited for the ambulance.

How could anyone think she'd done that on purpose?

A quiet sob slipped from her throat.

"Morgan?"

She lifted her head from her knees, spotted Quinn's tall, muscular frame in the doorway and swiftly lowered her head again. "Go away," she mumbled.

For a man who'd been in the army for five years, he wasn't good at taking orders. Instead of leaving, he strode into the room, crossed the thick burgundy carpet with long strides and was on his knees in front of her chair before she could even blink.

"Hey," he murmured. One warm hand reached out to cup her chin and tilt her head up. "What's going on?"

"Nothing." She tried to shrug out of his grip. "Just crazy little Morgan with her behavioral issues and delusions."

He chuckled. "Self-pity does not become you, sweetheart. Now come on, tell me what happened."

She gave up trying to push his hand away, because he'd begun stroking her jaw with one long finger and it felt far too good. Kneeling before her, he was so close she could smell his woodsy aftershave, his natural spicy scent, his oddly sweet shampoo. She went on sensory overload, breathing him in, basking in the warmth of his hand on her tear-streaked face.

I miss you, she wanted to say.

Instead, she said, "Tony called. Like everyone else, he thinks I was alone on the bridge, so drunk and upset I decided to drive off it." She swallowed hard. "Oh, and he thinks I should go on medication."

"That's ridiculous." Quinn held her chin with two fingers and forced her to meet his gaze. "You're not crazy, Morgan."

"Maybe I am. Maybe I did imagine the other car."

"Do you honestly believe you hallucinated what happened?"

"No," she admitted after a moment. "But crazy people don't know they're crazy."

"Crazy people also don't question their own sanity," he said practically. "Jeez, sweetheart, you're the sanest person I know. If anyone's nuts, it's me, for flying off into the jungle and getting my ass shot at."

She managed a smile. "Brave, not nuts."

"Well, you're brave, too." His green eyes softened, making her want to throw her arms around him and never let go. It was so rare, seeing that tenderness in his eyes. "You've stood strong against the press and the rumors and the accusations for years now, and not once did you break. Don't let them break you now."

"It's easy to ignore the media, or even the people in town. But my own brother thinks I'm insane, Quinn."

Quinn shook his head. "Tony's only worried about you. He loves you. He's just so easily influenced by the senator."

"Who isn't?" she said sullenly.

His gentle fingers traced the line of her jaw, sending a flurry of shivers up her spine. Their eyes locked for a moment, and his head dipped ever so slightly. Morgan's pulse sped up. Would he kiss her? She suddenly longed for the feel of his mouth on hers, for the familiar rush of pleasure and love that filled her body each time their lips met.

With heavy-lidded eyes, Quinn's gaze lowered to her mouth. His lips parted. Morgan's eyelids fluttered closed in greedy anticipation for his kiss.

It never came.

Her eyes popped open as Quinn cleared his throat. Before she could blink, he was on his feet and utterly expressionless. "Why don't you grab those files and meet me in the living room?" he said briskly. "I want to bring myself up-to-date on the case before we head out tonight."

He left the study without another word, while she stared longingly after him, wishing desperately that he had kissed her.

"So, this is everything I have on Layla's disappearance." Morgan averted his eyes as she dropped a thin stack of files on the glass coffee table in the living room.

Quinn was grateful she wasn't meeting his gaze. He didn't want to look into her beautiful blue eyes, and see the hurt and disappointment he knew he'd find there. Damn it, he'd almost kissed her again. So close, he'd come so close, and yet he stopped himself just in time. He couldn't succumb to the temptation, no matter how appealing she was, no matter how vulnerable she'd looked with her smooth, creamy skin stained with tears and her eyes awash with pain and frustration.

Lord, he needed to tamp down this foolish attraction. Nothing good could come out of it. They'd failed miserably the first time around, and he wasn't about to give it a second go. He was no longer the angry, messed-up kid who couldn't understand why everyone around him had abandoned him. At thirty-two, he understood perfectly. You couldn't trust any-

ody but yourself, couldn't rely on anything but your own
ill and perseverance.

No matter how much he was still attracted to Morgan, he
efused to let her cast her spell on him again.

Leaning forward, he reached for the first file folder, opened
and found a photograph of a pretty brunette staring back at
im. He'd seen the picture before, instantly recognizing Layla
imms. She'd been an attractive girl, with long, shiny brown
air, deep hazel eyes and a smile that could light up an entire
om during a power outage.

Beneath the photo were some high school transcripts, and
medical file he wasn't quite sure he wanted to know how
iorgan had gotten her hands on.

Morgan joined him on the pristine black leather sofa,
eping a good two feet between them. She picked up another
lder and pulled out a single sheet of paper. "This is Jake's
atement," she explained, frowning at the mere mention of
e sheriff. "Colin Kincaid, the deputy who rescued me from
ie river, gave me some copies of the police files when I first
arted investigating, before Jake became sheriff." Her frown
eepened. "Now I can't get access to anything."

Quinn took the paper from her, scanned it, then raised one
yebrow. "Jake was the last person to see her alive?"

Morgan nodded. "That's why he's on the top of my suspect
ist. According to Jake, he saw Layla in the field behind the
igh school."

"She looked 'flushed and nervous, like something was
otally bugging her,'" Quinn recited from the statement.

According to Jake, Layla then hurried off in the direction
of the path leading into the woods. Apparently the Phys. Ed.
teacher often made his students jog along the trail in the forest,
so Jake wasn't worried that Layla was going alone. Like most
of the other students at Autumn High, she would know her
way around, as long as she kept to the trail.

"Think she was meeting someone in the woods?" Quinn speculated.

Morgan's eyes took on a thoughtful glint. "Possibly. Or she could have been going for a run. Jake said she was wearing sweats and a tank top, which she usually wore when she exercised. The two of us used to jog that trail often."

"So what are you thinking? Jake followed her into the woods, maybe hoping to get back together, they argued, he killed her, then buried her body in the forest?"

"Possibly," she said again. She made a sound of frustration. "We really need to get our hands on the autopsy report. I still have no idea how she was killed, and that could make all the difference."

"How so?"

"Well, if she was stabbed or shot, I can't see Jake being responsible. If she was beaten to death, on the other hand, that's right up Jake's alley. He picked so many fights as a teenager. Definitely used his fists instead of his brain."

"We'll have that report tonight," Quinn reminded her.

Morgan didn't respond. He glanced over and saw the uncertainty pooling in her bottomless blue eyes. "What's wrong?" he asked gruffly.

"What if we never find the truth?" Her forehead creased with unhappiness. "I've spent ten years on this case. I don't know how much more I can take."

"We'll find the truth."

"You really think so?"

The hope suddenly shining in Morgan's eyes sent a surge of determination through him. When she looked at him like that, her beautiful face filled with hope and trust and desperation, he was ready to give her any damn thing she wanted. Morgan hated showing vulnerability, and when she did, it melted his freaking heart.

Annoyed with how easily he let her get to him, Quinn set his jaw and looked down at the file in his hand. But he could still feel Morgan's gaze on him, the need for reassurance pouring out of her and seeking him out.

He would be a real ass not to offer that reassurance.

Lifting his head, he met her gaze and in a resolved voice said, "We'll find the truth, Morgan. I promise."

Chapter 8

Rather than parking Quinn's SUV at the high school, they left the car in the parking lot of an all-night diner a block away, then walked to the school. It was past midnight, and Morgan shivered in the late night air, wishing she'd brought a pair of gloves. Quinn, of course, wore black leather gloves that matched perfectly with his black trousers, sweater and boots. She'd donned an all-black getup too, yet on Quinn, it looked natural, while she resembled a Catwoman-wannabe. Make that cat burglar. With her wavy blond tresses tucked under a black wool hat, she looked precisely like what the people in town thought her to be—someone about to cause trouble.

"It's so cold," she grumbled as they crossed the field behind Autumn High and headed for the woods. "I even have goose bumps on my butt."

Quinn shot her a sideways glance. "Thanks for sharing."

The dry quip raised her spirits slightly. It wasn't the "can I see it?" he would've lobbed her way two years ago, but it wasn't quite a "shut the hell up," either. Ever since the almost kiss they'd shared in her study, she hadn't been able stop thinking about how much she wanted it to be more than *almost*. She'd found herself staring at his mouth all evening, to the point that her brain had turned into a hazy pool and she hadn't been able to concentrate on anything else.

She'd dated a few men before she met Quinn, but nobody had ever compared to him. His intensity, his rare smiles, that dry sense of humor and brooding strength... She loved everything about him. More than that, she respected him. It was difficult finding a man in D.C. who wasn't all about appearances, ambition, getting ahead. Yet Quinn didn't give a damn what people thought of him. He was tough, rough and utterly composed. Nothing got to him.

You did, a little voice pointed out.

Yeah, she'd gotten to him in more ways than one, hadn't she? By his own admission, she was the only woman he'd ever loved.

And she'd broken his heart.

"Here's where the trail starts," she said, pushing away her distressing thoughts as they approached the woods.

A muddy, twig-strewn path bisected the trees. She experienced a tremor of apprehension as she stared at the shadowy trail, suddenly wishing she'd had the foresight to bring a flashlight. Fortunately, the Boy Scout at her side pulled one out, flicked it on and pointed the faint stream of light at the darkness.

"I'm surprised Jake didn't post a guard here," she said, glancing around the empty field warily.

"You never know," Quinn said with a shrug. "There could be someone waiting for us at the scene."

He was wrong. After they walked half a mile or so into the dark forest and reached the roped-off area where Layla's remains had been found, nobody jumped out from the trees to surprise them. Yellow crime-scene tape isolated a square of forest, surrounding a shallow makeshift grave. The police had excavated the grave after a jogger's dog dug up—Morgan cringed—Layla's skull. A pile of dirt sat next to the gaping hole.

"Oh, Layla," she whispered, approaching her best friend's final resting place. She slowly turned to Quinn. "She didn't deserve this."

"No, she didn't," he replied softly.

Without hesitation, Morgan ducked under the yellow tape and knelt beside the grave. She stared at the dirt, unable to fathom how anyone could have done this to Layla. Killed her, buried her here. Wild foxes and coyotes were frequently spotted in the area, and Morgan felt nauseous at the thought that a wild animal could have chewed on Layla's bones as if she were nothing but a late-night snack.

She swallowed the bile creeping up her throat and stood up abruptly. "There's nothing here," she said, desperation lining her tone.

Quinn, who'd been examining the surrounding area, glanced over. "It's been ten years. Any blood, or trace evidence, would have been washed away long ago. If that dog hadn't decided to explore this stretch of woods, her body would have probably stayed buried for who knows how long."

Morgan brushed dirt off her knees and joined him, shaking her head in anger. "I want to find out who did this, Quinn. I owe it to Layla and her family."

"You'll find the truth," he said.

"I hope so." She tore her gaze away from Layla's grave and straightened her shoulders. "Come on, let's head over to Davidson's office."

They didn't speak as they followed the trail back to the high school. Morgan thought of Layla, conjuring up the memory of her mischievous eyes and hundred-watt smile. Layla was the only true friend she'd had. The other girls at school, snooty girls like Beth Greenwood, loathed Morgan, probably because Edward Kerr practically owned the town. They never ran out of nasty things to say about her. If she showed up to school in a new outfit, they called her a rich bitch. If she went out on a date, she was a slut. If she was too distracted to say hello to someone in the hall, she was a snob.

But not Layla. Layla didn't care how wealthy Morgan's family was, and unlike the others, she hadn't been jealous of the wealth either. That's what Morgan loved most about her, the down-to-earth nature, the complete lack of interest in trivial matters like popularity, or envy, or jealousy. Layla had been a first-class friend.

"Should we drive to the M.E.'s office, or walk?" Quinn asked when they reached the parking lot where they'd left the car.

"Drive," Morgan replied. "The medical complex has a back alley where we can stash the car."

The trip to Frank Davidson's building took all of five minutes. Autumn was a small town; almost everything was within walking distance, save for the Kerr estate, which was a fifteen-minute drive from Main Street. Morgan always suspected her father's family had built the mansion so far from town on purpose, so the lowly townsfolk wouldn't find it so accessible. Ironic, since every Kerr politician, including her father, based his campaign on being a people-person, accessible to everyone around him.

Davidson's office sat adjacent to Autumn's medical clinic, a fact that had always creeped her out as a kid. She'd be seeing her doctor for her annual checkup, and thinking about the dead bodies next door the entire time.

Quinn parked the car in the alley and killed the lights and engine. For the first time all night, he cracked a smile. "Bring your lock-picking kit?" he teased.

She reached into the inner pocket of her black coat and retrieved the small, leather case. "Sure did."

"All right, let's see if you remember what I taught you."

His words brought a smile to her own lips. She still remembered that night as if it were yesterday—Quinn patiently teaching her the basics, then handing her the tools and letting her have a go at every lock in her apartment. Once she'd even picked the lock in her father's office, just to see if she could.

"That was, what? Our third date?" she teased back. "I doubt that's proper dating etiquette, buddy, teaching your date how to behave like a criminal."

"Picking locks is a skill everyone should know," he answered with a shrug. "What if you ever got locked out of your apartment?"

"That's what landlords are for."

"And if the landlord isn't there that day?"

She sighed. "Unlike you, I don't think that far ahead."

He grinned again. "No kidding. Your impulsiveness is your fatal flaw." He paused thoughtfully. "And on the other hand, it's one of your best traits. Figure that one out."

Warmth spread over her body like a loving caress, and she averted her eyes before he could see the longing she knew must be flickering there. She wasn't one for redundancy, but damn it, she missed him. Every five seconds, the thought came to her mind. She missed him. Missed him. Missed him. And she couldn't help it. She'd thought about Quinn every day for the past two years, and now that he was finally here, she couldn't stop the floodgates from opening. Everything about him brought back familiar feelings of love and heat—and damn it, she *missed* that.

Forcing aside her thoughts, she got out of the car and the two of them crept toward the steel door in the alley. Her pulse sped up a little as she removed two small tools from her kit and bent over the lock. Quinn stood behind her, shielding her from view as she inserted a hook pick into the lock and started fiddling around. The telltale click of the lock's inner cylinder came so fast she couldn't help but twist her head to shoot Quinn a huge grin.

"Still got it," she whispered.

His mouth twitched. "Nice job, Kerr."

She slid up to her feet and pushed the door handle. The moment they stepped into the shadowy corridor, the alarm mounted on the wall began to beep, warning them they had ten seconds to enter in the code before the alarm started shrieking like a banshee.

"My turn to shine," Quinn murmured. He swiftly stepped up to the panel, retrieved a wire cutter from his pocket and made a series of snips to the wires hooked into the control panel. The beeping instantly stopped.

"How do you know which ones to cut?" she asked curiously.

"This is the cheapest, most common model on the market," he said, gesturing to the panel. "It's the first model I ever learned to bypass."

"What'd you do, do an internet search for Bypassing Alarms 101?"

"Nah, bought a copy of *Alarms for Dummies*," he said glibly.

She rolled her eyes, then shifted back to business mode. She pointed to the open doorway at the end of the hall and said, "That's the morgue. Davidson's office is upstairs."

They headed for the morgue first, where Quinn approached the wall of refrigerated metal compartments. He studied the identification stickers on each section, pausing in front of one at the far end. "She's here," he said quietly.

Morgan's throat tightened as Quinn tugged on the handle and pulled out the stretcher containing Layla's remains. She'd visited morgues before, on other assignments, but the sight of her best friend's bones brought her perilously close to vomiting.

"You okay?" Quinn asked, catching her eye.

She sucked in a gulpful of oxygen, willing the nausea away. "I'm fine."

Reluctant, she stepped forward and studied the skeleton lying on the cold metal. She tried to pretend she was looking at something in science class, a random set of bones that didn't belong to anyone she knew. Just an anatomy lesson.

The bones hadn't been bagged and labeled yet. Morgan wished they had. It was highly disturbing looking at her friend's skeleton laid out on the table, faded gray bones assembled to form a crude version of a former human being. The bones were surprisingly preserved, though. Other than a scary set of tooth marks on the fibula bone, most likely from a hungry animal, the skeleton presented very little damage. Little *natural* damage, that is.

Quinn let out a soft whistle. "I think we know cause of death."

She rounded the table and went to his side, gasping when he pointed out the deep depression in Layla's skull. Without touching anything, he moved his finger over the skull to highlight the evident trauma. "Two fractures here," he pointed out. "And see how this part of the skull is nearly caved in? I think she died from a blow, or multiple blows, to the head. We should peek into Davidson's files for confirmation, but there doesn't seem to be damage anywhere else."

Morgan stared at her friend's fractured skull for a long moment, into the pair of gaping eye sockets that seemed to be glaring at her.

She turned away as a wave of pain crashed into her body with the force of a tsunami. "She was beaten then," she choked out. "Something Jake is quite capable of doing."

"Let's check if we're right." Quinn slid the remains back into the compartment, then took her arm.

She stood frozen in place, her gaze glued to the metal cubicle. "We can't just leave her here," she said, looking at Quinn in anguish.

He slowly led her toward the door. "Yes, we can. Layla isn't here, Morgan. It's just her bones. She's been gone for a very long time."

She knew he was right, but she couldn't bear the thought of Layla lying in that ice-cold hole in the wall. Blinking back tears, she followed Quinn up the narrow set of stairs leading to Davidson's office. This time he picked the lock, and a few minutes later, they grabbed Layla's file from the filing cabinet near the desk.

"Subdural hematoma," Quinn confirmed as he scanned the medical examiner's report. "Says here he suspects she was hit numerous times in the head with a blunt object. A rock, he speculates."

A lump of fury clogged her throat, making it difficult to speak. "Someone bashed her head in," she choked out. "God, how could anyone to do that?"

Quinn sighed and placed the report back in the cabinet. "There are some pretty messed-up people in this world, sweetheart. You know that better than anyone."

Yes, as a journalist she'd come across some sick people over the years, but that didn't lessen the pain pulsing through her body. "We need to go to Jake's office," she said decisively.

Quinn didn't seem enthused. "I still think it's a bad idea. What do you expect to find, a signed confession in his desk drawer? I doubt the sheriff would keep any incriminating evidence in his office."

"He might," she countered. "Jake isn't the sharpest tool in the shed. Maybe we'll find something."

Although Quinn didn't look hopeful, he humored her, and ten minutes later, they sneaked into the small police station through the back doors. The cells in the holding area were empty, not surprising considering Autumn didn't boast many criminals, save for a few drunken locals hauled in to sober up. Oh, and a seventeen-year-old girl's killer, who still roamed the streets.

Jake's office was on the second floor. Despite the late hour, the building was lit up like a Christmas tree, and Morgan could hear the faint voices of the deputies stationed at the front desk on the main floor. She and Quinn crept toward the stairwell. She winced when the door handle clicked as Quinn opened it. Fortunately, the chatter of the deputies continued on without pause.

Outside Jake's office, Morgan went for her lock-picking kit again, but realized she didn't need it. The sheriff's door was unlocked.

"If he had something hidden in here it would be locked," Quinn said so softly she barely heard him.

Ignoring his words, she crept into the office, waited a moment for her eyes to adjust to the darkness, then made a beeline for the desk while Quinn stood watch at the door. None of the desk drawers were locked, and to her disappointment, none of them contained anything important. She went to the filing cabinet next, which Jake had actually bothered to lock. Shocking. It took a few seconds to pick the lock, and then she was flipping through the alphabetical files until she found Layla's name.

"Unbelievable," she huffed as she scanned the meager report. "This is exactly what I have at home, the files Deputy Kincaid gave me *ten* years ago. Nobody's even touched the case since then!" She frowned. "All Jake did was add the M.E.'s autopsy report."

Quinn chuckled. "Are you surprised? Sheriff Wilkinson didn't strike me as the go-getter type. His entire investigation probably consisted of opening that cabinet and sticking the M.E.'s notes into it."

"Yeah, because he's probably the killer," she grumbled as she closed the filing cabinet. "Why bother investigating a murder you committed?"

Quinn let out a breath. "You know, I think it might be more fruitful if we focused on finding out who came after you on the bridge. This case is too cold, the evidence too sparse. If we look for the person who tried to kill you, we'd have a better chance of—" He stopped abruptly, cocking his head.

Morgan heard the footsteps at the same moment as Quinn.

"Crap," she muttered. "We need to hide."

Before the word *hide* even left her mouth, Quinn was pulling her toward the tiny bathroom in the corner of the room. He shoved her inside, closed the door and pressed her against the wall. "Not a sound," he whispered into her ear.

Yeah, like she was even capable of making a sound when he had her pinned to the tiled wall with his big, firm body. His proximity made her pulse take off like a racehorse, fast, sharp beats drumming in her ears and stealing the breath from her lungs. His spicy scent wafted into her nose, making her dizzy, aroused.

When a shivery breath escaped her lips, Quinn shot her a warning look. "Quiet," he murmured.

Okay, she could be quiet. Just ignore his intoxicating nearness, and the delicious hardness of his chest against her aching breasts, and the—

"I'm just picking up a file I forgot," came Jake's voice.

Morgan could hear the sheriff moving around the office, his heavy footsteps, the sound of papers rustling. He was obviously on his cell phone, and his muffled voice held a note of irritation as he said, "I told you I would call you when I got home. You didn't need to leave seven messages on my voice mail, damn it."

A pause, more papers being shuffled, then a low curse. "I already told you, you don't need to worry about Morgan."

Morgan's body stiffened at the sound of her name. She stared at Quinn wordlessly. They both frowned.

"She's not going to find out, okay?" Jake sounded even more aggravated now. "She's only in town for a few days, and the senator promised he'd find a way to make her leave if she stays too long. We've managed to keep this secret for years now. We can handle a few more days."

Jake paused again. "No, that's not a good idea. It's late. You'll raise suspicion." Another beat. "Fine, tomorrow night then. Ten o'clock at Grady's cabin. We'll figure it out then, okay?"

The person on the other end of the line must have found this satisfactory because the argument ceased. But not before Jake yet again reiterated the words that sent a chill up Morgan's spine. "She won't find out. I'll make sure of it."

Chapter 9

"We have to be at that meeting," Morgan announced when she strode into the living room the next afternoon.

Quinn glanced up from the book he was reading with a stern look. "Haven't we been through this already? Following the sheriff tonight is a bad idea."

He'd given her this lecture three times already, once on the drive back to the mansion last night, and twice earlier today. They'd gotten home at three in the morning yesterday, and Morgan had slept in until past noon. She'd woken up alert and determined, knowing she had to follow Jake to his meeting with the mysterious caller, only Quinn was less enthused.

"I don't trust the guy," he said yet again.

"Neither do I, but that's exactly why we need to follow him tonight. You heard him on the phone last night. The secret he was talking about? It's obviously that he's hiding the fact that he killed Layla."

Quinn looked dubious. "And what, he's got an accomplice? The evidence suggests it was a heat-of-passion kind of murder.

Someone got pissed off and beat her to death. I can't see two people gathering together to smash her skull in."

Morgan winced at his callous words. "Maybe there are two killers. Or maybe not. Maybe Jake got drunk one night and confessed to the person on the phone. We won't know unless we follow him."

"This could be a trap."

"Jake isn't bright enough to orchestrate traps," Morgan replied with a roll of her eyes. She flopped down on the leather sofa next to him, causing the pages of his book to rustle. Curious, she glanced at the title. "*The History of Panama*? Jeez, can you get any more dull?"

He ignored the insult and said, "The guys and I might be heading down there in a few months, so I figured I'd do a little research. And don't give me that look, I found the book in your library, so someone in this house is evidently as dull as I am."

His remark sparked her curiosity. "Why are you going to Panama?"

Quinn's green eyes became shuttered. "I've been hearing some talk of trouble in one of the villages. A contact of mine mentioned we might need to extract some of the relief workers there if all hell breaks loose."

She tried not to let the revelation concern her, but Quinn's assignments always brought a pang of worry to her stomach. Although he kept an apartment in D.C., where they'd once lived together, he'd gone out on missions several times in the two years they were a couple. And from the moment he said goodbye, until the moment he called to say he was coming home, all she did was fret. Pray he would stay safe. That he would come back to her.

And yet…yeah, there might have been some envy along with the anxiety. The magazine usually assigned the more dangerous stories to seasoned journalists, but on a few rare occasions she'd been allowed to go overseas. The assignment in the Congo, where she'd met Quinn, had been the last time she'd traveled to a hot zone, and sometimes she longed for a little more excitement, some danger.

She suddenly burst out laughing, a sharp unexpected sound that had Quinn glance over at her like she was nuts. "Did I miss the punch line?" he asked, raising his dark brows.

Morgan giggled again. "No, it's just…I was thinking about how I wish I could go on more overseas assignments, you know, have some danger and excitement in my life. And then I remembered someone tried to kill me last week. You'd think that would be enough danger to satisfy me."

Something indefinable flickered across his face.

"What?" she prompted.

He gave a shrug, averting her inquisitive gaze. "Nothing. I was just thinking how difficult it is to satisfy you."

Suddenly the air in the stuffy living room grew even stuffier. Swallowing, Morgan awkwardly rested her palms on her thighs and said, "What's that supposed to mean?"

Quinn finally brought his gaze back to hers. Bitterness clouded his eyes. "It means exactly what it sounds like. You're a hard woman to satisfy. God knows I tried." He sucked in a breath. "And failed, of course."

Confusion flooded her body. "You didn't fail," she protested. "*I* failed. I'm the reason you left, Quinn."

His voice grew hoarse. "I left because I obviously wasn't enough for you, Morgan. You weren't satisfied with just me, with our life."

"Yes, I was." She blinked back the tears threatening to spill over. "I loved our life together."

"Not enough." His powerful chest heaved as he drew in another breath. "You chose your other life over ours. Your role as the senator's daughter instead of Adam Quinn's fiancée."

The pain in his voice made her heart ache. A part of her also felt an inkling of irritation, because evidently he still refused to understand why she'd agreed to her father's request to postpone the wedding. It wasn't because she loved Quinn any less. Her father had been up for reelection, and she'd promised her mom she would stick by him when he needed her. She told all this to Quinn, the night she asked to delay their wedding until after her dad's reelection, but he hadn't understood where she was coming from.

"I wanted to marry you," she whispered. "I just wanted to push back the wedding for a few months."

Quinn shook his head, looking irritated. "You know that's not the only reason I left, Morgan. Your father was sticking his nose into our business long before you asked to delay the wedding." He snorted. "Our dinner reservations, our vacations, the goddamn brand of toothpaste we used—he interfered with every aspect of our lives."

"I tried to get him to back off," she protested.

Quinn frowned. "Evidently not hard enough."

"You know my father, Quinn. He's determined to get his way about everything…" She trailed off when she realized he wasn't interested in her excuses.

"I made a mistake," she whispered. Her chest felt as if someone had scraped it open with a razor. "And I've regretted that mistake every day for the last two years, okay?"

He didn't respond, but the animosity in his eyes dimmed slightly, giving her the nerve to continue. "I miss you," she admitted. "I think about you all the time, Quinn."

His features softened, just a bit, and her courage rose even higher. Her hand shook as she lifted it to his face, fingers trembling wildly as she gently stroked his strong jaw. He winced at the touch, but didn't draw back. His breaths came out ragged, and Morgan could see the battle raging in his eyes. Lust and anger. Hurt and anticipation.

God, it felt good touching him. The pads of her fingers brushed across the five o'clock shadow on his cheeks, relishing the feel of him, the sharp planes of his face, the fullness of his bottom lip. Her heart pounded so loud she was surprised he didn't comment on it. When she slowly slid her hand from his jaw to his neck, and then his chest, she could feel his heart beating, too, thudding against her palm.

His large, warm hand suddenly covered hers, impeding her tentative caresses. "You should stop," he growled.

"Why?" she murmured. "You can't tell me you don't like me touching you. You know you've missed me as much as I missed you."

His green eyes flashed. "Damn it, Morgan. I don't want to play these games with—"

She kissed him before he could finish that sentence. And what do you know, he kissed her back, with such passion the oxygen drained from her lungs and a wave of dizziness crashed over her. His taste was familiar, the feel of his lips against hers like a homecoming, yet there was something different about him, too. An edge, a roughness that troubled her and excited her at the same time.

His mouth and tongue were relentless, toying with her, claiming her. When his hot tongue slid into her mouth, she whimpered, and he swallowed the desperate sound and deepened the kiss. The air around them grew thick, the sizzle of sexual attraction flowing freely from her body to his like a bolt of lightning looking for a place to strike.

Morgan threaded her fingers through his dark hair, stroked the nape of his neck, touched his jaw, desperate to make contact with him. And his hands were doing some exploring of their own. He cupped one aching breast over her thin cashmere sweater, the heat of his hand searing right through the material and making her nipple jut out against his palm. He squeezed, fondling one breast, then the other, until she was moaning in his arms.

Yet it wasn't enough. She shifted restlessly on the couch, sliding closer to him, rubbing against his rock-hard thigh. "I need you," she choked out. "God, Quinn, I need you so much."

He froze for a moment, and when her eyelids fluttered open she immediately saw the hard look in his eyes. She knew she'd said something wrong, did something wrong, but Quinn didn't give her time to question his sudden harshness.

One hand abruptly left her breast and reached for the fingers she'd tangled in his hair. Green eyes glittering with arousal and another emotion she couldn't quite label, he gripped her hand with his and dragged it to the waistband of her gray wool slacks.

Letting go of her hand, he deftly unbuttoned her pants and peeled them off her legs, leaving her sitting on the leather couch in nothing but her skimpy black panties. Then he took her hand again and, before she could object, placed it directly over her core.

Morgan gasped from the intimate touch. It didn't matter that it was her own warm palm pressing against her throbbing sex. The contact caused a rush of pleasure to spiral through her body and settle between her legs.

"See, you don't need me," Quinn said in a hoarse voice, covering her hand with his again.

In the back of her mind, a warning bell sounded. He was playing with her, toying with her so he could…so he could what? Make a statement? Prove a point? Yet the gentle stroking of his fingers—*her* fingers—overpowered the apprehension. Her entire body grew achy and agitated, her breasts heavy with arousal, and every soft brush of her own finger against her clit made her gasp.

"That's it," Quinn muttered. "Let's see how much you need me."

He continued directing her movements, moving her hand over her damp panties, pressing down on her fingers when he decided she wasn't applying enough pressure. Morgan struggled to breathe. She wanted to push him away, tell him to go to hell for whatever game he was playing, but she couldn't find the willpower. She could feel the climax building, and there was no stopping it. It had been so long. Too long. And regardless of whose hand it was between her legs, it was Quinn's presence sending her closer to the precipice. Quinn's masculine scent, and raspy breathing, and—*oh, yes*. Release pounded through her body, a combination of soaring pleasure and aching pain that fragmented her mind and thundered through her body. Burst after burst of ecstasy exploded inside of her, until she finally slumped back against the leather sofa cushions, gasping for air.

Very slowly, Quinn lifted his hand, leaving only her own pressing against her pulsing center. He stood hastily, but not before her glazed eyes took in the obvious erection straining against his faded blue jeans.

He made no mention of his arousal. He just stared at her, rueful, aroused, bitter. "You don't need me." he said again, squaring his broad shoulders until he stood like a stiff marble statue in front of her. "Next time the thought enters your mind, remember you're perfectly capable of making yourself feel good. As you can see, you don't need me for that."

Shaking his head to himself, he stalked out of the room, leaving her sitting bewildered on the sofa.

"You arrogant bastard!"

Quinn paused at the foot of the majestic spiral staircase, stifling a sigh. He'd known it wouldn't take her long to shake off the aftereffects of the climax and let the fury take over. And hell, she deserved to be mad. He'd acted like a heartless son of a bitch back there, and he wasn't proud of it. Yet hearing her utter those words—*I need you*—had unleashed a storm inside of him.

She'd proven two years ago that she didn't need him. Didn't want him. He'd wanted to remind her of that. Sure, he might have gone about it the wrong way, but the truth remained the same. Morgan had tossed him aside, and just because she suddenly decided she wanted him around again didn't mean he would pull her into his arms and pretend the past hadn't happened.

"What was that about?" she continued, charging across the marble floor and intercepting him before he could take another step. "You wanted to prove a point, was that it?" Her blue eyes flashed. "Well, you proved nothing."

He tried to ignore how beautiful she looked, with her cheeks flushed from climax and anger. Instead, he pasted on an indifferent expression and said, "I proved that you don't need me."

"Why, because I had an orgasm?" she shot back. "I've got a news flash for you, Quinn, *you* made it happen. I climaxed because you were there with me."

Oh man, why did she have to say the word *orgasm?* The erection he'd been attempting to get rid of returned with full force, jutting against his zipper. He ached for her, *craved* her, and he hated himself for the traitorous reaction. He'd had two years to get over his desire for her, and he thought he'd succeeded. But from the moment he'd laid eyes on her back at their cabin, he'd been in a constant state of arousal.

"What exactly do you want from me, Morgan?" he asked, slowly meeting her gaze.

She faltered, as if she'd expected him to lash out again and didn't know what to say now that he hadn't. "I want…" Her voice drifted for a second, and then she cleared her throat. "I want *you.*"

His hard-on jerked against his jeans but he refused to give it the attention it pleaded for. "Morgan—"

"I want your forgiveness," she added, turning her head, but not before he glimpsed the sorrow swimming in her blue eyes.

He let out an uneven breath. "I forgave you a long time ago."

Her gaze flew back to his. "What?"

"I forgave you," he repeated.

"So, why…" Her delicate throat bobbed as she swallowed. "Why are you fighting the attraction? You know it's still there, Quinn."

"It is," he agreed quietly. "But that doesn't mean I'm going to act on it. I'm through with relationships. I have no interest in getting involved again, with you, or anyone else."

Her voice became soft. "That's foolish, Quinn. You're just going to shut yourself off from everyone for the rest of your life?"

He shrugged. "I have my job, my guys, I don't need anything else."

She shook her head. "I never took you for a coward."

"There's nothing cowardly about this," he replied, nearly cringing at the defensive note in his voice. "I've just decided I prefer being alone."

"Because of me." She sagged against the railing of the staircase. "I hurt you, and now you're reverting back to the man you used to be before we met, the one who refused to open his heart to anyone."

Annoyance seized his insides. "Don't psychoanalyze me, Morgan. The way I feel about relationships is none of your concern, not anymore. I'm here to help you find out who tried to kill you and figure out what happened to your friend. That's all I'm equipped to do."

Her eyes rested briefly on his groin, which still sported an erection that refused to go away. "It looks like you're equipped for other things as well."

His irritation grew. "What are you suggesting exactly? You want me to take you to bed?"

"Yes."

Her candid response threw him for a loop. "For God's sake, why? I just told you I'm not interested."

"In *relationships*," she said. "You didn't say a word about casual flings."

Despite himself, he laughed. "You honestly think, after

everything we've been through, that anything between us could ever remain casual?"

"It can if we keep it that way."

He wavered for a moment, disgusted when he realized he was actually considering this ridiculous proposal. He chalked it up to the fact that he hadn't had sex in two years, but *that* reminder only evoked another wave of disgust. He'd almost gone to bed with someone else, a cute redheaded tourist he met in Venezuela six months after he left Morgan, but the entire encounter had been awkward and frustrating. Unable to get Morgan out of his head, he ended up leaving the redhead in her hotel room with a confused expression on her face.

So yeah, he was a little hard up for some physical action.

But not with Morgan.

Because really, how could he possibly have sex with her after he'd made love to her?

"Forget it," he said flatly.

Disappointment bloomed on her face. "There's nothing wrong with giving in to the attraction between us."

"There's plenty wrong with it." He sighed. "Let's just drop this, all right? Are you still determined to spy on the sheriff tonight?"

His swift change of subject obviously caught her off guard, but she recovered quickly. "Yes, I am."

"Fine. Then wake me up at nine-thirty. I'm taking a nap until we leave."

He attempted to continue up the stairs, but she blocked him again. "So that's it?" she taunted. "You're going to pretend nothing happened between us in the living room, that the conversation we just had didn't exist, and just tail the sheriff tonight?"

With a grim nod, he moved her aside with a little more force than necessary and ascended the stairs. "That's precisely what I'm going to do," he called over his shoulder.

* * *

Quinn never got around to that nap, though he did stay out of sight until it was time to head out. He made a few calls, stared at the walls of the guest room and did his best to ignore the sound of Morgan's footsteps roaming the main floor.

She truly was nuts, but not in the way her father claimed. A casual fling? As if the two of them could ever manage something *casual*. They were too explosive together, the passion too strong, the emotions too raw.

He chuckled to himself. Casual. Ha.

Although he still thought following the sheriff to his mysterious meeting with his possible accomplice was a bad idea, Quinn didn't have much of a choice in the matter. Morgan would go whether he accompanied her or not, and considering her hotheaded nature and animosity toward Jake Wilkinson, Quinn wasn't in the mood to bail her out of jail tonight.

Throwing on a dark blue sweatshirt, he headed downstairs with a sigh. Morgan was waiting in the foyer, tapping her foot impatiently. She'd changed into a pair of jeans, a dark sweater and hiking boots.

"Planning on climbing a mountain?" he asked.

"Grady's cabin is in the middle of the woods. I can't go in heels."

"Wait, you know where this place is?"

"Of course." She grinned. "There's only one Grady in town, and he happens to be a good friend of Jake's."

They exited the house and walked toward the car, neither of them mentioning the fiery encounter they'd had mere hours ago. Quinn hadn't expected Morgan to bring it up. Knowing her, she was biding her time, letting the proposition sink in before she raised the subject again. And she would raise it, of that he was certain. When Morgan wanted something, she didn't stop until she got it.

And at the moment, apparently she wanted him.

He gulped and pushed away the thought. Out of habit, he

opened her door, waited until she climbed in, then rounded the vehicle and hopped into the driver's seat.

"So what's the story with this Grady guy?" he asked as he drove through the gates. "Why does he live in the woods?"

"Because he's weird." She leaned back in her seat and folded her arms in her lap. "His name is Grady Parker, and he was in my grade in high school. He didn't have a lot of friends, yet somehow he and Jake were buddies, which was odd since Jake was a jock and jocks hate everybody that isn't a jock."

"You're rambling."

"Oops, sorry." She shot him a sheepish smile. "Anyway, Grady was always scribbling away in this ominous black notebook—I think he might have been plotting our deaths. Seriously, he had school shooting written all over his face—"

"Rambling again."

She scowled at him. "*Anyway,* he didn't go to college, just got a job at the lumber mill in Huntersville, the next town over. He has no friends, doesn't go out much. His parents died a few years ago, so now he lives in the family house, which, like I said, is in the middle of the woods. There's a small cabin on their property, a few hundred yards from the big house, and I think that's where Jake is heading. Make a right up there."

Quinn followed her directions, turning onto a narrow road heading north. He tapped his fingers on the steering wheel, thoughtful. "Pot or moonshine?"

Morgan glanced over. "Huh?"

"Grady is a weird recluse who lives in the woods, has no friends and keeps to himself. He either grows pot, or makes his own moonshine—which is it?"

From the corner of his eye, he saw her fighting a grin. "Pot," she replied. "I'm pretty sure he dealt drugs to Jake in high school. Grady's dad apparently had a grow-op somewhere on the property."

As they reached the tree-lined driveway leading up to the

Parker house, Quinn decided there was no "apparently" about it. Parker was definitely engaged in some illegal activities. On each side of the driveway were bright red signs with the words TRESPASSERS WILL BE SHOT written in large block letters. Normal people didn't put up signs like that. Pot growers, on the other hand...

When they passed the third death-threat sign, Morgan gestured for him to stop. "The main house is right up there. We'll walk the rest of the way so he doesn't see us pulling up," she said.

Quinn steered the SUV off the path and parked it near the trees, then killed the engine. The clock on the dash read ten-twelve. They'd intentionally arrived after the rendezvous time so they could be sure Jake was already there. "All right, let's get this over with," Quinn grumbled.

They left the car and Morgan led the way into the woods. Despite the carpet of twigs underfoot, Quinn's boots didn't make a sound as they walked through the brush. Years as a mercenary—and the army tours before that—had taught him to blend into the shadows and keep his presence hidden until he was ready to reveal himself. Years of experience had also taught him to recognize any sign of danger, and within two minutes in the woods, he sensed they were being watched.

Morgan, on the other hand, chattered away obliviously. "Tony and I used to sneak out here when we were kids. We were convinced Grady's dad was either in the Mafia, or else a spy for—"

"Quiet." Quinn lifted his hand to silence her, his senses on high alert.

Morgan fell silent immediately, a nervous glint in her eyes.

He scanned the area, noticed a faint beam of light up ahead, and made out the vague shape of a small, A-frame cabin. The locale of Sheriff Wilkinson's mysterious meeting. But the threat he sensed wasn't coming from that direction. No, someone was in the trees, somewhere behind them. Other than the soft sound of the night air and the rustling of tree branches, the woods were silent, yet the back of Quinn's neck tingled, signaling they had company.

As he opened his mouth to order Morgan to keep her head down, the crack of a rifle broke through the still night. Without hesitation, he launched himself at Morgan and pushed her to the cold earth, just as a bullet whizzed over their heads.

Chapter 10

Fear, combined with a rush of sheer adrenaline, slammed into Morgan's body at the sound of the gunshot. She pressed herself to the dirt, the weight of Quinn's body against her back both comforting and terrifying. Someone had shot at them! Still shooting, in fact, she realized as another gunshot roared in the night. A bullet connected with a nearby tree, shattering the bark and sending a branch crashing to the ground.

She squeezed her eyes shut and covered her head with her hands, praying for the shots to cease. A moment later, they did, and the woods became ominously quiet.

Morgan tried to move out of Quinn's grip, but he held her down. "Don't move," he whispered into her ear, his warm breath tickling her neck.

"I think it's over," she answered.

"Not likely," he muttered.

He was right. Though the bullets were no longer flying above them, Morgan suddenly heard the sound of twigs breaking.

Her heart thudded against her rib cage. Whoever had shot at them was coming closer. Her panic escalated, then faded into relief when she heard a gruff voice snap, "Get off my property."

She recognized Grady Parker's voice instantly. The fear drained from her body like bathwater, replaced by a sharp pang of irritation. "What the hell are you doing shooting at me, Grady?" she demanded, wiggling out from under Quinn and sitting up.

Her former classmate blinked in surprise. "Morgan?"

"Yes," she retorted as she rose to her feet.

Quinn got up, too, and she noticed him eyeing the other man with distrust. She understood his reaction. Grady Parker didn't look like the kind of man you'd willingly hand your trust to. Tall and lean, he had sharp angular features that made him appear almost feral, pale gray eyes and a thick black beard. He wore a flannel jacket and a black ski cap, and held a long rifle in his gloved hands.

The expression on his face, however, was sheepish. "I didn't know it was you," he told her, as if that excused the fact he'd almost blown her head off.

"Do you shoot anybody who walks onto your property?"

Grady bristled. "The signs are here for a reason. I don't like trespassers."

Unlike most of the other people in town, he didn't speak to her in a tone reserved for mental patients. Although they hadn't been friends in high school, Morgan had always been pleasant to the eccentric loner, and he'd remembered that kindness over the years. A couple of years ago, when she was home for a visit, they even shared a cup of coffee at Jessie's Restaurant.

But gunfire wasn't part of their tentative acquaintance-ship.

"Well, maybe find out who's trespassing before you start shooting," she shot back. "You could have killed us."

Suspicion filled his gaze. "Why *are* you trespassing?" He glanced at Quinn in distaste. "And who's he?"

"This is Quinn, my…" She faltered, then said, "A friend of mine. And we're not trespassing. We're here to see Jake," she lied.

Grady's fuzzy black eyebrows soared. "He knows you're coming?"

"Of course." She avoided Quinn's eyes. No doubt he was sporting a look of supreme disapproval. "Though I'm not sure why he said to come to this cabin. Does he use it often?"

Something resembling amusement crossed Grady's gray eyes. "Often enough," he replied, his lips twitching. He paused, tilting his head. "Are you sure he told you to meet him here?"

"Yep," she said smoothly.

"Huh. All right. I'll walk you over there then."

Grady tucked his rifle under his arm and moved in the direction of the cabin, looking over his shoulder to make sure they were following. Morgan stepped after him, but Quinn locked his hand on her arm and forced her to pull back.

"What the hell are you doing?" he muttered. "Jake has no idea you're here, and he's not going to appreciate you following him."

"I couldn't tell him we were spying on the sheriff," she hissed back, shrugging his hand away. "Just go with it."

Quinn didn't answer. She could tell he was ticked off, but she ignored the stormy look in his eyes. She knew what he was thinking—they'd planned on hiding in the woods and spying on Jake to see who he met with, and now that plan had gone to hell, and Quinn wasn't happy. But what other choice did they have? She hadn't planned on getting caught by Grady, or confronting Jake tonight, but both those items were obviously on the agenda and they would just need to adjust.

"So, uh, how are you doing?" Grady asked, shooting her a curious look over his shoulder. "I heard about the accident."

"I'm fine." She shrugged. "You know me, nothing keeps me down for long. Not even a trip to the bottom of the river."

Grady's harsh feature softened. "Layla's service was tough, huh?"

She swallowed. "Yeah, it was."

"She was such a nice girl," he said. "I hope they find the son of a bitch who killed her."

That's why I'm here.

She kept her thoughts to herself, instead nodding in agreement and ducking under the branch Grady held up for her. He let the branch go just as Quinn approached, nearly clocking the other man in the head, but Quinn's wilderness survival skills far surpassed Grady's. He moved under the branch swiftly, not even breaking his stride.

The trees thinned out, and the trio stepped into a small clearing, where a log cabin, not unlike the one Morgan had once shared with Quinn, sat on a patch of dead grass. The large window at the front of the cabin was lit up like Christmas Eve, a pale yellow glow seeping through the dark curtains. And the narrow front door gaped open, revealing the bulky frame of Autumn's sheriff, who'd obviously heard the gunshots and come out to investigate.

Jake charged down the rickety porch steps when he spotted them entering the clearing. His dark eyes burned with anger. "What the *hell* are you doing here?" he spat out, glaring at Morgan, then Quinn.

Grady swiveled his head at her. "I thought you said he was expecting you."

Morgan offered a sheepish smile. "I may have exaggerated a little."

Despite her admission of a lie, Grady seemed unperturbed. Instead, he shrugged and said, "I'll let you three hash this out. I've got soup on the stove in the big house." Still holding his rifle, he walked off in the direction they'd come from, leaving Morgan and Quinn alone to face Jake's wrath.

The sheriff looked absolutely livid, but there was also an odd glimmer of embarrassment in his eyes, which should have sparked her curiosity if she weren't far too distracted by his attire. Or lack of.

Jake was bare-chested.

Huh. If he were meeting an accomplice, why on earth would he take off his shirt?

Realization dawned at the precise moment another figure filled the open doorway of the cabin.

"You've got to be kidding me," Morgan muttered.

"Jake?" Beth Greenwood descended the porch wearing nothing but tiny black shorts and a skimpy pink camisole that clashed horribly with her red hair. "What's going on?"

Beth's green eyes darkened the moment she spotted Morgan. "What is *she* doing here?"

"That's what I'd like to know," Jake muttered. He gave Morgan a harsh scowl. "Well?"

"We followed you," she said with a shrug.

Her words brought another turbulent flash to Jake's eyes, but it was nothing compared to how he'd look if she admitted they broke in to his office and eavesdropped on his phone call. A phone call she'd *totally* misinterpreted.

"You followed me," he echoed. He faltered. "That's impossible. I never saw a tail."

Quinn offered a pleasant smile. "What can I say? I'm good."

Jake sneered at the other man, then bestowed the same gift on Morgan. "I can arrest you for this," he told her. "This is harassment."

"You're not going to arrest us," she said, rolling her eyes. "If you do, tonight's activities will come to light, and I doubt you want that to happen." She shot a pointed look at Beth's scantily clad figure.

Beth placed her hands on her curvy hips, her gaze hurling

daggers at Morgan. "What is your problem?" she demanded. "Why do you have to be such a nosy bitch?"

Morgan didn't flinch at the insult. "I'm just trying to figure out who killed my friend. Is that so hard to grasp?"

"Finding the killer is my concern," Jake snapped. He crossed his arms over his bare chest, his massive pecs flexing.

"And you're doing a lousy job of it," she shot back. "Instead of investigating, you're holed up in this love shack with a married woman. Does Travis know about this?"

Beth paled at the mention of her husband. "He doesn't," she said coolly. "And if you say a single word to my husband, I will kill you."

Jake silenced Beth with a grim look. "Stop," he ordered. "It's pointless flinging threats at each other." His voice suddenly sounded strained. "Seriously, Morgan, what do you want?"

"I want to find the truth," she said simply. "And I don't want you standing in my way."

He frowned. "And I suppose if I tried to stop you, you're going to tell everyone what you saw tonight?"

Swallowing, he glanced over at Beth, and Morgan was stunned by the tenderness in his eyes. Oh, brother. Was Jake actually in love with her? Didn't he know that he was most likely just another notch in Beth's already very long belt?

Jake must have caught the sympathy in her eyes because he let out a sigh. "We've been seeing each other for five years."

The revelation sent her eyebrows soaring to her hairline.

"Travis has no idea," he continued, "and we intend to keep it that way."

To Morgan's surprise, Beth's green eyes filled with tears. "He's got a heart condition, and this would destroy him." She gulped a few times, obviously fighting back sobs. "He began to suspect a few years ago, so I tried to divert his suspicion by starting some rumors about me and, um, other men. The rumors were so ridiculous, even Travis couldn't believe them, and he thinks Jake was a rumor, too."

Morgan gave her former classmate an incredulous look. "You mean *you* spread all those rumors that you were getting involved with every man who passed through town?"

Beth's voice sounded very small, and very wistful. "I couldn't let Travis find out about Jake. Travis and I have three children together. We have a history." She sighed. "But we haven't been in love since high school." Beth looked over at Jake, her eyes shining with adoration. "Jake is the only man I love now."

A spark of guilt burned a hole in Morgan's belly. Next to her, Quinn was utterly expressionless. He had barely said a word all night, save to voice his disapproval over her impulsive plans, and she suddenly wished they'd done things his way tonight. It felt wrong, witnessing Jake and Beth's unmistakable affection for each other, and with Jake's eyes so gentle and soft as he looked at Beth, he suddenly didn't look like a killer.

Morgan drew in a breath. "Did you kill Layla?" she finally asked, her quiet question directed at the sheriff.

He met her eyes, holding the gaze for a long moment. "No, I did not kill Layla."

His voice held a note of conviction and truth, which made Morgan release the breath she'd been holding. Damn it. He wasn't lying to her. She had a sixth sense when it came to these types of things, and right now, she was convinced Jake Wilkinson had nothing to do with her best friend's murder. The secret he'd hinted about during the phone call…he'd been trying to hide his affair with Beth. Not his role in Layla's death.

Which meant this entire night had been nothing but a wild-goose chase. Not to mention a grave invasion of privacy.

"Will you let me dig around to see if I can figure out who did?" she asked.

Jake's stocky chest heaved as he let out a heavy breath.

"Morgan, I wasn't lying to you when I said I've been investigating. But there's nothing to find. The case is too cold. There are no suspects. No evidence. Nothing."

"Maybe so, but I'd like to find out for myself."

Jake's hand slid down to grasp Beth's, his fingers tightening over hers. "Will you keep this to yourself if I give you my okay?"

She would have kept their relationship to herself regardless, but she nodded anyway. "Yes. I promise."

"Then fine," he said briskly. "Dig around. But I guarantee you won't find anything. I don't think we'll ever know who killed her."

"Maybe," she said again. "Maybe not."

A short silence fell, broken by the sound of the wind hitting the metal shutters on the cabin's front window. There was a chill in the air, bringing goose bumps to Morgan's body and making her realize it was getting late.

"We should go," she said to Quinn.

He nodded in stony agreement.

She glanced at Beth and the sheriff. "I'm sorry we intruded on you two tonight." Her voice cracked. "But Layla was… she was important to me. I need to know what happened to her."

To her complete shock, Beth reached out and lightly squeezed her arm. "You'll figure it out," the redhead said, her voice unexpectedly reassuring and lacking all its usual venom.

Morgan met the other woman's eyes and cleared her throat. "Thanks, Beth. And don't worry, your secret is safe with me." She turned to Jake. "If my father calls you…"

Jake wrapped one bare arm around Beth's slender shoulders. "I'll assure him you're not interfering with the investigation and say there's no pressing need for you to return to Washington."

Relief coursed through her. "Thank you."

* * *

"Do you believe him?" Morgan asked as they drove away from Grady Parker's property and headed home.

Quinn nodded. "I don't think he killed Layla."

A sigh rolled out of her throat. "Yeah, I don't think so either. Which means we need to come up with a new suspect. Let's go over the case file again when we get back."

"Sure." Quinn kept his gaze on the dark road ahead, nonchalantly adding, "And maybe we can also discuss your complete disregard for your own safety."

The remark was meant to be casual, but the moment he said it, the memory of what happened back there in the woods assaulted his brain. The hiss of the bullet as it shot past Morgan's head, the feel of her small body beneath his, fragile, vulnerable. She could have died. If the person who'd run her off the bridge had been in the woods tonight instead of Grady, she *would* have died.

The fear crawling around in his chest made his lips tighten. Damn it. This was precisely why he'd originally wanted to tell the senator to go to hell when he asked for Quinn's help. He didn't want to worry about Morgan. Because of her impulsive nature, he'd done a lot of worrying when they were together, always on edge when she took on a particularly risky assignment. *World at Large* was tame as far as magazines went, the journalists on staff usually focusing on the political scene and the occasional human interest piece. But not Morgan—she always chased the dicey stories, the ones that sent her headfirst into danger.

He knew a part of it had to do with proving herself. Hell, she'd only gotten the job because a friend did her a favor, and she'd spent years trying to show the editors she was more than the flighty daughter of a senator. So she took risks. Sometimes they paid off. Other times…

Quinn was suddenly tempted to reach across the seat and shake some sense into her. "What if Grady shot you?" he burst out. "I told you I didn't think it was a good idea following Jake tonight, and instead of listening, you charge into the situation blind, and get us shot at."

She seemed unperturbed by his harsh tone. "Grady wasn't aiming to kill. He just wanted to scare what he believed were trespassers." She raised one dark blond eyebrow. "And don't tell me you haven't been shot at dozens of times before tonight."

"I have," he agreed, "but I'm trained for this kind of thing. You, on the other hand, aren't. If I hadn't pushed you down, you would have stood there, chattering away, while a bullet connected with your forehead..." He trailed off suddenly, slightly frazzled by the thickness of his voice, the raw note of distress that Morgan would certainly pick up on.

And she did. Sucking in a breath, she stared at him in surprise. "You were concerned about me. Scared for me." Wonder lined her tone.

"Yeah, so?" he grumbled.

Her delighted laughter filled the suddenly hot car. "So, it's nice. You've kinda been acting like a jerk since you stormed back into my life, and it's good to know a part of you still cares, even just a little."

A little? God, he wished that were true. But he had the unsettling feeling that his feelings for Morgan ran deeper than "a little." Two years apart, and he still hadn't gotten her out of his system. She'd only been back in his life for two measly days, and already she was under his skin again.

"I care, too," she added, so softly he strained to hear her.

Flicking on his signal, he turned onto the road leading to the Kerr estate, wishing his pulse hadn't raced when she said those words. *I care.* Other than the guys he worked with, there weren't many people who cared about him. Not that he was whining about it. Hell, he'd come to the conclusion a long time ago that sometimes you were better off the fewer people who cared for you.

"I thought about you a lot these last couple of years," she went on. "I worried about you."

He glued his eyes to the road. If he met her gaze, he knew he'd see a myriad of emotions in her big blue eyes. Emotions he wasn't ready to face yet. If ever.

"You shouldn't have," he said gruffly. "You know I can take care of myself."

"Like you took care of yourself in Johannesburg?"

He furrowed his brows. Now how in the hell did she know about—

"Murphy called," she said, her throaty voice trembling.

Quinn's fingers tensed around the steering wheel. "That nosy, presumptuous son of a—"

"Don't be angry with him."

Her warm hand suddenly reached out and covered one of his. Quinn nearly let go of the wheel, then forced himself to stay calm. He steered through the mansion's gates and parked in front of the pillared entrance. He could've pushed her hand away when the car came to a stop, but he didn't. God help him, but her touch felt too damn good.

"He called when you were in the hospital," she said, gently tracing his knuckles with her index finger. "He said you'd been shot while rescuing the ambassador's daughter and that you lost a lot of blood. He wanted me to fly out."

Quinn slowly turned to meet her gaze. The worry he saw in her eyes touched him, the disapproval made him want to smile. "But you didn't."

She swallowed. "No. I thought about it, but I knew you wouldn't appreciate it. You told me to stay out of your life, so I did."

The stab of regret he experienced from her words bugged him. She'd chosen her father over him, and the way he saw it, he had every right to say those words. So why did the idea that he'd hurt her make his heart ache?

"Murph probably exaggerated the injury," he said, trying to keep his tone light. "It was just a bullet to the thigh."

"Hitting the femoral artery," she replied stiffly.

Quinn couldn't help but grin. "It was nothing. Seriously, Morgan, don't look so horrified."

She curled her fingers over his, her blue eyes suddenly searching his with such intensity the grin on his face faded.

He wrinkled his brow. "What is it?"

"I should have come," she whispered. "I agonized about it for hours. I even had the phone in my hands so I could make a flight reservation. In the end, I chickened out. I couldn't bear having you look at me that way again."

"What way?" he asked, then wished he hadn't.

"As if you hated me."

A twinge of regret floated around in his gut. "I never hated you. I loved you, even when I ended it, I still loved you." He shook his head ruefully. "It took me two years to get over you."

She let out an unsteady breath, her fingers trembling against his. For a moment she just stared at him, then slowly pulled her hand back and pressed it to her knee. "You got over me?"

He met her eyes and said, "Yes."

It was a lie. The past two days proved that he had definitely, irrevocably, *not* gotten over her. He still ached for her, still craved her, but telling her the truth would achieve nothing. When he'd said he wasn't interested in relationships any longer, well, that *hadn't* been a lie. He'd lived a solitary life these last couple years, and he liked it. Relationships had always been difficult for him; even with Morgan, he'd never quite felt like he was cut out for it, but she'd dazzled him with her wit and laughter and spontaneity, to the point where he believed he might be able to make a marriage work.

But when she canceled their wedding, he realized the truth. His childhood had screwed him up beyond repair. He would always want too much out of a relationship, expect his partner to meet the unbelievably high standards everyone else in his life had previously failed to meet.

In a way, Morgan had done him a favor. Made him see that he was better off alone.

"I don't think you're telling the truth." Her unhappy voice drew him from his thoughts.

He sighed. "You just don't want to believe it."

Her perceptive blue eyes studied him again. For a few long moments, their gazes locked, until Morgan finally shook her head and broke the eye contact. "Let's go inside," she said.

He didn't like her complete lack of expression, or the dull note to her voice, but he wasn't going to push her. Whether she believed him didn't matter. Whether he was over her didn't matter, either. They had no future, and that's all that mattered.

Unbuckling his seat belt, Quinn got out of the car and followed Morgan to the enormous front doors. She rummaged in her purse for her keys, then pulled them out and reached to unlock the door. She froze just before the key made it to the lock.

She pointed to the ground. "Was that there when we left?"

Quinn glanced down warily. Sitting on the porch directly next to the front doors was a white, letter-size envelope. No postmark, no sender or return address.

"No, it wasn't there." He knelt down and picked up the envelope by one corner, then rose to his feet. The envelope wasn't sealed, and when he held it under the porch light, he saw it contained a lined piece of paper, the kind kids stuck in their school binders.

"Should we open it, or take it to the police?" Morgan asked.

Quinn rolled his eyes. "The police? You mean Jake? Considering he seems to spend more time sleeping with a married woman than doing his job, I think it's safe to say he won't be much help with this. Let's open it."

Morgan stared at the envelope as if it were a bomb. "You do it."

He smiled faintly. "Yes, ma'am."

Neither of them spoke as he gently lifted the flap and extracted the paper, again only grasping the corner. Chances were there would be no prints, but one could never be too careful.

He noticed Morgan's hands shaking again, the glow of the porch light illuminating the flicker of apprehension in her eyes. Slowly, he unfolded the paper.

There were only two words on the sheet, each one cut out from a newspaper and glued on the paper creepy serial-killer style. Only two words, but they spoke volumes, and sent a chill up Quinn's spine.

Leave town.

Chapter 11

"What does it say?" Morgan demanded.

Without a word, Quinn handed her the note. Trepidation crept up her spine as she lowered her gaze to the paper. The two words brought a spark of fear and anger. "What the hell does this mean?" she asked.

"I think it means whoever wrote the note wants you to leave town," Quinn said helpfully.

"Duh." She rolled her eyes at him. "But why? Is it a threatening kind of leave town, as in, *leave town or I'll kill you?* Or is it a helpful warning, you know, *leave town because you're in over your head and as a concerned citizen I think you should go?*"

Quinn's lips twitched. "I highly doubt a concerned citizen would take the time to cut individual letters from a newspaper and glue them to paper. A phone call would probably make more sense."

"So it's a threat then."

He nodded, a deadly glint filling his eyes. "Yeah, I think it is."

She unlocked the door, deactivated the alarm and bent down to unlace her boots. "Who do you think sent it?" she asked as she watched Quinn kick off his own boots.

"I'm assuming the person who killed Layla."

Ice filled her veins. "Do you think he'll come after me again?"

"Or she," he pointed out. "We have no idea if it was a male or female who killed her."

"What do you think?"

"Male," he admitted. "The fractures in her skull indicate the attacker was very strong." He grinned. "And before you say women are strong, too, I know that. The nature of the crime, though, leads me to believe it's a man."

"Me, too." She stood up, opened the large closet in the front entrance and shoved her and Quinn's boots inside. "I need to be more careful." She bit her lip. "You realize whoever left that note somehow managed to get through the gates. There's a code you need to punch in, Quinn."

"I know." He shot her a rueful look. "But you know how easy it is to bypass anything electronic these days. You saw how quickly I disabled the alarm at Davidson's office."

He was right, it probably wouldn't be that hard to circumvent the gate. The interior alarms, though, would pose a serious problem for whoever delivered the note, which was probably why he—or she—left it on the porch.

"I always told my father we should have security cameras set up outside," she remarked. "He thought the system inside was enough. But if he'd listened to me, we would be able to see who dropped the note off tonight."

"It is a pretty good interior system," Quinn admitted, his gaze straying to the keypad on the wall. "Motion detectors, sensors at every door and window. It would be difficult for an intruder to break in to this house."

"But not impossible," she said, fear rising in her throat.

"No, not impossible," he agreed. He noticed her concerned expression and shot her a reassuring smile. "Don't worry, even if someone managed to break into this fortress, they wouldn't get past me."

"No?" She lifted one eyebrow. "Grady got past you tonight."

Quinn shot her a bewildered look. "I knew he was following us."

"You did?"

"Of course."

"So why did we wind up facedown on the dirt? You weren't even armed."

The corner of his mouth tugged upward. "Says who?" Before she could respond, he lifted the hem of his sweatshirt and did a half turn, revealing the gun tucked into his waistband.

Despite the ominous view of the weapon's sleek black handle, a rush of heat flooded Morgan's body. He'd lifted his shirt, and the smooth strip of golden-brown skin exposed made her mouth go as dry as a desert. God, she wanted to touch him. She remembered how soft his skin felt beneath her fingers. He didn't possess an ounce of fat, only sinew and muscle and sheer masculine power.

Morgan gulped, trying to bring some moisture back into her mouth. It didn't work, so instead she tried to focus on the reason they were together in the first place. The case.

"I'm going to find who killed her, Quinn. I don't care if Jake says the case is too cold." Ignoring the pulsing waves of desire in her body, she made for the study. "We're going to pore over those case files until we come up with a new lead."

"*You're* going to," came Quinn's dry voice from behind.

She paused at the end of the foyer. "You're not going to help?"

"Not tonight. I plan on taking a shower, going to bed and

looking at those files with fresh eyes in the morning." He shrugged out of his black coat as he spoke, tucking it under his arm.

"Suit yourself," she said. Determination hardened her features. "But I'm staying up."

"Suit yourself," he mimicked. His green eyes suddenly softened. "Don't stay up all night. Layla will still be dead in the morning."

The remark, though gently delivered, sent a shot of pain to her chest. "I know."

He studied her for a moment, as if he wanted to say something more. In the end he just sighed. "Good night, Morgan."

"Good night, Quinn."

She watched him climb the winding staircase. When he disappeared from view, she headed for the study. She'd left the files on her desk, a thin stack that for ten years had failed to result in a single viable lead. Her back muscles ached as she sank into the leather chair, making her realize she'd hit the ground a lot harder than she'd thought.

The memory of Quinn's body shielding hers brought another infusion of warmth. She wished he'd been on top of her for another a reason, one that involved a bed and a healthy dose of lust, not danger.

But apparently he'd gotten over her.

Yeah, right. She'd lived with the man for two years, long enough to become adept at reading every expression, every nuance…every lie. And he'd lied to her out in the car. He still wanted her.

With a sigh, she reached for the first file, which contained the interviews the former sheriff conducted when Layla went missing, but before she could open the folder, the phone on the desk began to ring. A glance at the caller ID revealed the line to her father's D.C. penthouse.

The sigh became a soft groan. Well, she shouldn't be surprised her dad was calling. It had been two days since she'd left the hospital. She was surprised he'd held out this long.

Gearing herself up for what she knew would be a fight, she picked up the receiver and leaned back in the chair. "Hi, Dad."

"Hello, Morgan." The senator's voice was so chilly she found herself shivering. "Are you ready to put an end to this madness and come home?"

"What madness are you referring to? My need to figure out who tried to kill me? My determination to solve my best friend's murder?" She shook her head to herself. "How can either of those things be considered mad?"

Her father ignored the sarcastic response. "The press broke the story of your suicide attempt. My PR team has been fielding calls since yesterday."

"So? They should be used to cleaning up my messes by now," she said with a bite of hostility.

"Aren't you growing tired of humiliating this family?"

Her fingers tightened over the phone. "You're the one who caused this, Dad. If you'd believed me when I told you about the other car instead of having me *committed,* the media wouldn't be salivating this way."

"I refuse to play along with your delusions, young lady," the senator snapped. "The sheriff investigated and found no evidence that someone ran you off the bridge. On the other hand, you've provided this family with *plenty* of evidence over the years showing you are unstable." He gave an uncharacteristic curse. "I want you to come home, Morgan. Tonight."

"Sorry, but no," she said through clenched teeth.

"Asking questions about your friend's death isn't going to achieve anything. The Simms girl is dead. It's tragic, yes, but it's been ten years. Even Mort and Wendy have let her go."

She wasn't buying the sudden softness of his tone. Her father always had an agenda, an ulterior motive, and he wasn't above using false kindness to get his way. Well, for the first time since her mother died, she wasn't caving in.

"I'm not leaving Autumn until I'm good and ready," she said evenly.

His gentleness faded so fast she almost laughed. And as usual, he tossed out the ace in his sleeve. The guilt card he never failed to use. "Your mother would be very disappointed in you, Morgan."

Ignoring the ache in her chest, which the mention of her mother always evoked, she set her jaw. "No, I think she'd be disappointed in *you*." Her throat tightened. "Mom would have believed me about what happened on the bridge."

"Your mother was always too naive," he replied curtly. "And apparently our friend Adam is equally naive. He was supposed to bring you home. Instead, he's buying in to your delusions."

"Quinn knows I'm not delusional, and I don't appreciate you contacting him behind my back." She swallowed. "Why don't you have any faith in me?"

Her father stayed silent for a moment. Then, rather than addressing the hurt-laced question, he said, "If you're not home by the end of the week, I'll take matters into my own hands."

"Nice, Dad, threaten me. I suppose you'll send some guys with white coats to take me to a padded cell."

She couldn't quite hide the pain in her voice, but as usual, her father remained oblivious to it. Or else he simply didn't care how much he hurt her. How much his lack of trust and faith had slowly chipped away at pieces of her heart over the years.

"The end of the week, Morgan," he repeated.

He hung up without saying goodbye.

Despite her best attempts at blinking them back, a few tears leaked from the corner of her eyes. Damn him. What would it take for him to show her an ounce of decency, an iota of compassion? She was his daughter, for Pete's sake, yet he treated her like a pawn he could move around his own little chessboard.

Her fingers shook as she placed the phone in its cradle. Breathing deeply, she wiped the tears from her cheeks, pushed back the chair and stood up. Layla's case files sat on the desk, pleading with her to look at them, but she couldn't do it tonight. Quinn was right. Better go over them tomorrow, with fresh eyes. After the conversation with her father, she was in no mood to search those papers for clues.

She shut off the light and left the study. She hesitated on the second-floor landing, the temptation to go to Quinn so strong her legs tingled.

She forced herself to keep walking. He might still want her, physically at least, but she knew he hadn't been lying when he said he didn't want a relationship again. She'd hurt him too badly two years ago, unearthed his old feelings of abandonment, and seeing as he was almost as stubborn as her, Quinn wouldn't back down on his newly resurrected no-relationship policy.

Which was a shame, because right now, she'd never needed anyone more.

In her bathroom, she took a quick shower, the warm water like heaven against her sore muscles. She got out, slipped into the tank top and cotton boxer shorts she liked to sleep in, then turned off the light and slid under the awful pink bedspread. Sleep. Sleep would make her forget…forget what? Everything, she realized as she shifted around under the covers, attempting to get comfortable. Quinn, her father, her brother, Layla, hell, even Jake and Beth…she just wanted to forget it all.

Only sleep never came. She tossed and turned, alternating between shutting her eyes and staring at the glaring red numbers on the clock by her bed. Just past midnight. Quinn was probably sound asleep, sprawled facedown on the bed in the guest room. His bare back long and smooth, his spectacular lower body covered by a silk sheet, his stubble-covered cheek pressed against the pillow.

Oh, God. She *ached* for him. Just imagining him lying in bed caused moisture to pool between her legs and made her nipples tighten painfully. She hadn't been with a man since Quinn. Hadn't wanted anyone *but* Quinn.

As if her arms and legs had a mind of their own, Morgan found herself pushing the bedspread aside and stumbling to her feet. The soft pink carpet tickled her bare toes, and she knew the hardwood floor in the hall would be cold, but she didn't pause to find her slippers. Her mind could only register one thing, and that was getting to Quinn.

Even as she stepped out into the dark hall, she realized how futile this was, pushing Quinn for an affair that would go nowhere. It was like getting friendly with the other passengers on the *Titanic* when you knew your fate ahead of time. What was the point? In the end you'd only wind up in the bottom of the Atlantic.

But damn it, she didn't care if she got wet, didn't care if she drowned when he left her again. Nobody in her life had ever cared about her the way Quinn did. He respected her, trusted her, made her feel special and appreciated and *loved*. Maybe he would take that love away in the morning, but at the moment, she didn't care. She needed it tonight.

Quinn was wide awake when he heard Morgan enter the guest room. He hadn't been able to fall asleep, just lay there in bed, staring up the ceiling and asking himself what the hell he was doing here. In Morgan's huge mansion. In Morgan's complicated life.

The second the door creaked open, he knew the answer to that question.

He was here for her.

"Are you awake?" she murmured.

"Yeah," he said thickly.

He slid up into a sitting position. His first impulse was to jump out of bed and get the hell out of there before things got out of hand. But he couldn't bring himself to do it. Instead, he searched the darkness until his eyes made out her shadowy figure moving across the room. She wore tiny green shorts and a loose gray tank top, her blond hair cascading down her shoulders like waves of silk. Those wavy tresses were tousled, as if she'd just woken up, but her alert blue eyes told him that, like him, she hadn't gone to sleep.

Her footsteps barely made a sound as she approached the bed. Quinn's entire mouth turned to cotton. She looked so achingly beautiful that his heart squeezed and his arms prickled with the urge to pull her toward him.

"What are you doing in here?" he asked, each word raspy thanks to the parched condition of his mouth.

"You know exactly why I'm here," she whispered.

And then she was on the bed. The mattress sagged slightly from her weight, then creaked as she climbed on top of him.

His pulse took off in a gallop at the feel of her soft thighs straddling his lower body. He hardened instantly, his erection rising up to press against her warm core.

Morgan gave a soft whimper at the intimate contact, then cleared her throat and said, "Let's get one thing straight."

He eyed her wordlessly.

"You lied to me before. You're not over me, just like I'm not over you."

"Morgan—"

She reached for the hem of her tank top, but didn't remove the shirt. "I'm not going to pressure you into a relationship," she interrupted quietly. "I promise I won't push you. I won't even ask for more than just this one night."

She began sliding the tank upward, pausing just before she revealed her breasts, which were bare beneath the cotton material. His gaze landed on her nipples, tight and hard, and a rush of desire swept through his body like a flash flood.

"But I need you to tell me you want me," she breathed, her voice shaky. "You have to say it."

Their eyes met, and for a moment he was floored by what he saw on her face. It shone with love and hope and regret, a whirlpool of emotions that both startled and thrilled him. It was rare, seeing Morgan look so vulnerable. It made him want to take her into his arms and never let go.

"Say it," she pleaded. "Please."

He swallowed the bittersweet lump lodged in his throat. "I want you, Morgan."

The admission should have made him feel weak, but the moment he said the words, a feeling of liberation soared inside him. For two years he'd locked up all his memories of this woman, banished her into a tiny dungeon in his heart that he never intended on opening. But it was open now, and all those old feelings flew out. All the old memories. All the passion.

With a groan, he clamped his hands on her slender hips and pulled her toward him. Their mouths came together so quickly, so intensely, that his lips actually trembled. He couldn't control the kiss, couldn't stop his tongue from thrusting into her mouth and claiming every inch of her.

She kissed him back with the same urgency, drowning him with her intoxicating taste, her sweet scent, her soft moans. And then she pulled back, her big blue eyes filled with desire and wonder, her breasts heaving as she drew in ragged breaths.

"I missed this," she confessed.

"Me, too," he murmured, then sucked in his breath when she lightly ran her fingers over his bare chest.

There was something very endearing about the way she touched him. Her caresses were smooth, skilled, as if she remembered every inch of his body and knew what drove him wild, and yet there was an awkward element to her touch, as if she were rediscovering him, too.

She dragged her palm over his skin, stroking his pecs, teasing his nipples. He let out a husky groan and reached for her, but she pushed his hands away. "Lie back and let me have some fun," she said with a twinkle in her eyes.

Have some fun? More like engage in a serious torture session. Quinn could barely breathe as she brought her lips into play, lowering her mouth to his chest and licking his collarbone. Her hot tongue slid over one flat nipple, sending a sizzle of arousal to his groin. After several excruciating moments, her tongue drifted south, following the thin line of hair that led to the waistband of his boxers.

"Take your shirt off," he said roughly.

Smiling faintly, she raised one hand and wagged a finger at him. "No way." Her smile widened. "I'm not through with you yet."

Chapter 12

Morgan's heart did a jumping jack at the arousal smoldering in Quinn's forest-green eyes. His pulse throbbed in his strong corded neck, a frantic *thump-thump* that told her he was enjoying her seduction as much as she was. Her gaze swept over his incredible chest, hard and smooth and dusted with light-brown hair.

She scraped her nails against his pecs, eliciting a husky groan from Quinn. His skin was scorching hot to the touch. She felt pretty feverish, too, especially when she glanced lower and spotted the thick erection straining against his boxers.

Licking her lips, she dipped her head again and kissed her way down to his waistband. Her hands hooked under the elastic and slowly peeled the boxers off his muscular legs. His arousal sprang up eagerly and even if the house spontaneously burst into flames, she wouldn't have been able to stop herself from touching him.

She curled her fingers around his shaft, squeezing gently. Quinn let out a moan, and a bead of moisture formed at his tip. With the sound of her pulse drumming out a tribal beat in her ears, she pressed her lips to him, planting a soft kiss on his engorged head before taking him into her mouth.

Quinn tangled his hand in her hair, guiding her, filling her mouth with his impressive length. She teased for a bit, alternating between soft licks and sharp pumps, until he moved restlessly on the bed, one hand clawing at the silk sheet.

"You're killing me," he choked out.

She lifted her head and smiled. The savage hunger on his face did indeed confirm she was killing him, but he'd also never looked more alive. Handsome features taut, eyes glittering with passion. He'd tried being aloof with her since they'd reunited, tried keeping his emotions hidden, but right now, in this amazing heated moment, everything he felt was written on his face.

She gave him one last kiss before sitting up. Quickly, she removed her tank top, tossed it aside, then shimmied out of her shorts and panties, which also found a place on the floor.

"You're beautiful," Quinn muttered, his heavy-lidded gaze moving over her naked body. He lifted one brow. "Is it my turn to have fun now?"

His words rang with sensual promise. Her body responded immediately, growing tense with anticipation.

"I suppose," she replied with a mock-indifferent shrug.

A crooked grin tugged at his mouth, and then, in the blink of an eye, Morgan found herself flat on her back with Quinn kneeling between her legs. His arousal was hot and heavy against her belly, and when she reached down to touch him again, he swatted her hand away.

"My turn," he reminded her.

She wasn't complaining. A shiver scurried through her as Quinn bent down and flicked his tongue over one nipple, which instantly grew even harder. He circled her areola with his tongue, then captured the rigid bud between his teeth and sucked it. Morgan squirmed, the painful arousal too much to bear. Her legs scissored beneath him, seeking his erection, pleading for completion, but he shifted so that his sex rested on her thigh, denying her what she craved.

Pleasure hummed through her body as he moved his attention to her other breast, licking, sucking, rubbing her nipple with his thumb. By the time he lowered one hand to her aching core, she was close to exploding. Flames licked at her naked skin, the fire growing stronger, powerful, then crackling into an inferno when he slid one long finger inside her.

She clamped her teeth down on her bottom lip, fighting the rising climax. It was no use. He pushed his finger deeper, then withdrew, pushed it in again, and the inferno exploded, hot waves of climax searing through her. Quinn drew her nipple into his mouth again, riding out the orgasm with her, his skillful fingers drawing out each burst of pleasure.

When she finally came down to earth, she noticed him putting a condom onto his thick shaft. "Where did that come from?" she croaked, her throat dry.

He smiled. "My wallet. You know I'm always prepared."

She was grateful he'd remembered protection, especially since she hadn't even thought about it. She'd stopped taking the pill after they broke up, so she was glad he hadn't forgotten about safety. Yet as he rolled the latex on, she experienced an odd flicker of regret. She almost wished he wouldn't, that they might start a baby tonight, so she could have something of his when he left her again.

Pushing aside the troubling notion, she wrapped her arms around his neck and pulled him down for a long, lazy kiss. Their tongues danced for a second, and then he was sliding into her, stretching her, filling her until she let out a sigh of pleasure.

"You're so tight," he muttered, spreading her thighs wider with his warm hands. He gave a hard thrust and buried his entire length inside her, then pressed his cheek to her shoulder, groaning quietly.

"It's been a long time," she admitted.

Quinn raised his head and searched her eyes. "How long?"

"Two years." She didn't need to elaborate. There hadn't been any other man since Quinn.

He let out a strangled breath and said, "For me, too."

Shock flooded her, but he didn't give her time to digest the information. He started to move, his pace fast and urgent, then slow and languid, each long thrust bringing her closer to the edge. She ran her fingers over the damp sheen of sweat on his back, closing her eyes and letting the sensations consume her. His hips started to piston, driving deeper, hitting a delicious spot that had her moaning uncontrollably.

They moved together in perfect sync, as if those two agonizing years apart had ceased to exist. Ripples of release gathered in her belly, spreading down to her sex and up to her tingling nipples, until the ripples formed a large, throbbing wave that finally crashed over her.

She cried out and buried her face against his solid chest, letting the pleasure take over. As she climaxed, his thrusts grew erratic, unrestrained, and suddenly he shuddered and let out a hoarse groan.

It took a moment for both of them to come down from the high the lovemaking had propelled them to. Morgan was breathing as heavily as Quinn, her breasts crushed under the weight of his chest, every inch of her quivering from the aftershocks of release.

Finally Quinn lifted his head and offered a wry smile. "Well, we're obviously still incredibly good at doing *that*."

A helpless laugh left her throat. "Yeah, we sure are."

He rolled off her and got up to dispose of the condom, while she lay back against the damp sheets, suddenly uncertain.

Would he ask her to leave? Announce his tremendous regret over what they'd just done?

He did neither. Turning off the bathroom light, he came back to bed and slid under the sheets, one strong arm pulling her toward him. She tucked her head against his shoulder and draped her arm over his chest. God, she suddenly felt like bursting into sobs, that's how wonderful it was being in his arms again. Her lips tingled with the urge to tell him she loved him, that she would always love him, but she feared it would ruin the moment.

Instead, she nestled closer to him, as he lifted the sheet over both of them and held her tighter. She fell asleep to the sound of his breathing and the feel of his fingers soothingly stroking her hair.

Quinn opened his eyes the next morning to the sight of Morgan's curvy, naked body sprawled on the mattress beside him. She slept on her side, facing him, with her silky blond hair disheveled and strewn across the pillow.

Despite himself, he smiled, loving how innocent and fragile she looked as she slept. He ought to have been frowning, because really, what the hell had he been thinking letting her seduce him last night?

You weren't thinking.

No, thinking hadn't played a part in yesterday's lovemaking. Feeling, that's what he'd been doing. Feeling her lips against his, her soft body beneath him, her tight inner muscles clamped over his—

He frantically attempted to reroute his brain but it was too late. His cock hardened at the memory, and he shifted uncomfortably, which unfortunately drew Morgan out of her slumber.

Blinking a couple of times, she finally opened her eyes and gave a tiny yawn. "Mornin'," she murmured.

Again he couldn't help but smile. Couldn't help touching

her, either. He stroked her bare shoulders, eliciting a sigh of pleasure from her. "That feels nice." She closed her eyes again. "Don't stop."

Although every logical part of his brain told him he *should* stop, his hands did the exact opposite. He ran his fingers up and down her back, gently kneading her muscles. Her skin felt hot and smooth beneath his palm.

He loved her body, her soft curves and small defined muscles. He moved his hand lower, dragging it over her round bottom. When he squeezed her buttocks, she let out a moan, then cranked one eye open and fixed him with a pointed look. "If you keep doing that, I'm going to want to get jiggy with it, you do realize that, right?"

He threw his head back and laughed. Damn, he'd missed her. Only Morgan could say things like "get jiggy with it" and not sound like a complete idiot.

"Maybe I want to get jiggy, did you think of that?"

She arched one perfect eyebrow and grinned. "What are you waiting for then?"

And yep, here was another thing he'd missed, her perpetual eagerness to get him naked. It had always given him a slight ego boost, how she never seemed to tire of him. She was always ready, always willing to give herself to him. And it was a two-way street. In the two years they'd been together, he hadn't tired of her, either. If anything, his need for her heightened each time they made love.

Sex, a sharp voice said. *Not love.*

Quinn swallowed. Right, he had to remember that. This…thing…between them had nothing to do with love. Whatever they felt for each other, well, it didn't matter. This was an affair, nothing more.

"Stop stalling," she teased, rolling over.

She arched her back, stretching it, and her breasts jutted out enticingly. There were faint red splotches on those luscious mounds, the result of his stubble chafing her delicate skin.

Call him crazy and primitive, but he liked seeing his mark on her.

"Seriously, Quinn, if you don't make a move I'm going downstairs to make some coffee."

"You'd choose coffee over me?" he mocked.

"Yep."

"Well, we can't have that, can we?" Leaning over the side of the bed, he rummaged on the floor for his wallet and fished out another condom. He had it on and was kneeling between her legs before she could even respond.

"Someone's a little overeager," she said with a smirk.

He wiped the smirk right off her face by sliding his shaft inside her. Two years of pent-up lust made it difficult to keep a slow pace, but he gave it a valiant effort, teasing her with languid strokes that had her moaning restlessly. The overwhelming desire torpedoing through his body shocked him, troubled him, but there was no stopping it. Morgan felt so warm and soft under him, her hair mussed up from sleep, her blue eyes glazed with what could only be described as bliss. This woman aroused him beyond belief, and it wasn't long before the lazy tempo he'd set transformed into a series of hurried, staccato thrusts.

Quinn slid his hands underneath her body, cupping her firm ass and lifting her so he could get deeper. But it wasn't deep enough. He wanted more, wanted all of her, wanted to bury himself so deep inside her and never come out. The all-consuming need startled the hell out of him. He tried battling it, pushing it away, but then Morgan wrapped her legs around him, dug her heels into his buttocks and he gave up fighting.

With a groan, he pumped harder, Morgan's breathy moans egging him on, bringing him closer and closer to the edge. And when he felt her muscles squeeze and contract, when he heard her cry of release, he promptly toppled right over that cliff. Pleasure seized his spine, searing a path to his groin and unleashing a climax so ridiculously powerful he lost the ability to breathe.

Gasping, he jerked inside her, burying his face against her neck. Her sweet feminine scent brought another spark of pleasure, her tight inner muscles milking him dry until he let out a hoarse breath and finally went still.

Christ. What just happened? The sex between them had always been good, but this…this was mind-blowing. He tried chalking it up to the fact that he hadn't gotten laid in two years, but he knew it was so much more than that.

It was Morgan.

Damn it, it had always been—and always would be—Morgan.

"Why haven't you been with anyone since we broke up?"

Her quiet voice sliced through his thoughts, and for a moment he wondered if she was a mind reader. No, she was just way too intuitive for her own good.

He withdrew gently and got rid of the condom, then slid up into an upright position and rested his head against the headboard. "Didn't have the time," he said lightly.

She sat up, too, wrapping the sheet around her body. The knowing glimmer in her eyes unsettled him. "You're lying again."

Quinn shrugged. "I guess I just never met anyone who interested me enough." He quickly turned the tables, anxious to get out of the hot seat. "Why haven't you been with another man?"

"I don't want another man," she said simply, meeting his eyes. "I've never wanted anyone but you, Quinn."

His throat went dry. He swallowed a few times, bringing much-needed moisture to his mouth. He'd intended to respond with a reminder that she shouldn't get attached to him again, but what came out was, "You never call me Adam."

Morgan looked startled. "What?"

Discomfort crept up his spine like ivy. "You don't call me

by my first name. Your father does, but he uses it to patronize me, or at least that's what it seems like. But you…" He cleared his throat. "You never use it."

She tucked her messy hair behind her ears and shot him an earnest look. "When we first met you told me you didn't like people using your given name."

You're not people, he wanted to say, but bit back the words. He had no idea where this was all coming from. He'd never given much thought to the fact that she called him Quinn. The only person who'd ever called him Adam had been his mother, the woman who abandoned him in front of a bank when he was five years old never to be heard from again. His father, who took off the year before his mother's departure, had called him "kid." Everyone after that just used his last name. *Quit fighting in school, Quinn. Clean your goddamn room, Quinn.* His foster parents had never addressed him as anything else, and over the years the name stuck.

So why did it suddenly annoy him to hear it from Morgan?

"I wish you didn't hate your name so much," she added, reaching out and touching his arm. "It's a great name."

He swallowed again. "It brings back some crappy memories, that's all."

"Do you want me to stop calling you Quinn?"

Her bewilderment increased his uneasiness. With a shrug, he swung his legs around and hopped off the bed. "No, forget I said anything. I think I'm still half-asleep."

He could feel her blue eyes focused on him as he retrieved his boxers and drew them up to his hips. Her confusion—and fascination—hung in the air, but he didn't say another word on the subject. He walked over to the window and parted the curtains, letting the pale morning sun stream into the room.

"Let's go make that coffee," he said gruffly.

Morgan nodded and slid out of bed, bending down to pick up her discarded shorts and tank top. He admired her lithe, curvy body as she dressed, wanting to kiss her but knowing it was probably a good idea if he kept his distance. Kissing her, touching her, would only send them right back between the covers.

He pulled his jeans over his boxers, left them unbuttoned. He didn't bother with a shirt, just followed her out of the room, his chest and feet bare. Morgan walked ahead of him, and he could tell from the slight tilt of her head she was still running their conversation over in her mind. Trying to figure out what the heck he'd been babbling about just now, no doubt.

Smothering a sigh, he trailed after her, surprising her—and himself—when he reached for her hand. She glanced at him for a brief second, puzzled, then laced her fingers through his and descended the steps. Neither of them spoke, but the silence was comfortable, even welcome.

The moment they reached the foot of the stairs, however, a startled curse broke through that silence.

Quinn swiveled his head just in time to see Morgan's brother Tony enter the foyer from the living room doorway. The other man's eyes, the same shade of blue as his sister's, widened at the sight of them.

Tony looked from Quinn's bare chest, to Morgan's skimpy night wear, to their intertwined fingers, and said, "What the hell is going on here?"

Chapter 13

Oh, brother. Literally. Morgan attempted to look calm and nonchalant as she met her brother's gaze, but within seconds, his disapproving blue eyes brought an embarrassed flush to her cheeks. She was a grown woman, yet under Tony's scrutiny she felt like a kid getting reamed out by her big brother.

"What are you doing here?" she asked, letting go of Quinn's hand.

"I came to check up on you. I was worried," her brother replied. His eyes became chilly. "But it looks like you're doing just fine."

She walked toward him, the marble floor like ice beneath her bare feet. Quinn followed her, hesitating for a moment before extending his hand toward her brother. "Hey, Tony, it's good to see you."

With obvious reluctance, Tony reached out and shook Quinn's hand then crossed his arms over his chest. Uh-oh, he had that stern, big-brother look in his eyes, which was almost comical, considering there was nothing stern about his appearance. He stood at a height of five-eleven, with a lanky frame and sandy-blond hair cut in a short, no-nonsense style. In his perfectly pressed khakis and sky-blue windbreaker, Tony looked like he belonged at a yacht club. He was so very different from Quinn, whose thick morning stubble and unruly dark hair gave him a lethal air.

"So it looks like I'm interrupting," Tony said, shifting uncomfortably.

Morgan managed a smile. "Not at all. We were about to make a pot of coffee."

"Why don't I go do that, while you two get dressed," Tony offered, a slight edge to his voice.

"Sounds great," she replied with fake cheerfulness. "Come on, Quinn."

They headed up the stairs, each to their respective floors. In her bedroom, Morgan took a lightning-quick shower, washing away the remnants of this morning's passion. She towel-dried her hair, then grabbed a pair of black trousers and a gray V-neck sweater from the walk-in closet and got dressed in a hurry.

Tony's visit was not going to be fun. Despite his claim that he'd been worried about her, she was fairly certain their father sent him to spy on her. And Tony was always ready to cater to the senator's whims. Sometimes she wondered where their close bond had come from. When they were kids, Tony had been closer to their mother. Idolized her, in fact. And although Morgan knew her mother loved her, Patricia favored her firstborn, and the two had shared a strong connection.

After her mom died, Tony had been inconsolable. He'd mourned her for months, letting his grades slip, withdrawing from his friends. He kept saying how their mother left him, how he was alone now, and it took him a long time to get over the loss. Apparently the senator helped him do that, because a year after Patricia passed, Tony seemed to transfer all his affection to their dad.

And Morgan, as usual, was the odd woman out. Stubborn, passionate, liberal and completely different from everyone else in the family, her late mother included.

She'd just buttoned up her slacks when a buzzing noise sounded from the door. It came from the intercom mounted on the wall, and when she walked over, she saw the button that connected to the kitchen was flashing. She pushed it and said, "I'm on my way down."

"Better hurry, coffee's getting cold," Tony's voice crackled back.

She couldn't help but smile as she left the room. When they were kids, she and Tony had a lot of fun with that intercom. It connected to every room in the house, and they used to go into opposite wings and have long, pointless conversations. Then they'd figured out that if you left a button pushed, the intercom stayed on, and they started eavesdropping on their parents, until their father finally caught on to what they were doing. Since then, the senator never entered a room without making sure the intercom wasn't on and relaying his conversations to the rest of the house.

Morgan headed for the kitchen, where she found her brother leaning against the black marble counter and sipping on a cup of coffee. Two other mugs sat on the counter, and he gestured to one. "I made it how you like it."

"Thanks." She crossed the pristine tiled floor and picked up the cup, breathing in the aroma of freshly ground coffee beans. She took a slow sip, letting the hot liquid slide down her throat, then made a sound of appreciation. "Oh, caffeine, how could I live without you?"

For the first time since he showed up, Tony cracked a genuine smile. "You need to cut down. You drink way too much coffee."

She rounded the counter and plopped down on one of the tall stools, still sipping away. "Maybe one day." She grinned.

"I was just thinking about how we used to spy on Dad with the intercom."

Tony laughed. "Oh, man, that was fun. Remember when we heard him talking to his publicist about whether he should start using Rogaine?"

She couldn't fight a giggle. "That was great. But then you made that comment about baldness at dinner and he figured out what we were doing. Way to spoil our fun, big brother."

Tony laughed again, then, holding his cup between both palms, tilted his head thoughtfully. "So…what's going on with you and Quinn?"

A sigh lodged in her throat. She pushed it down with another gulp of coffee. "Nothing serious," she said vaguely.

"Didn't look that way out in the hall."

Morgan set down her mug and met her brother's gaze. "Why are you really here, Tony?"

"I came to see if you were all right," he said, sincerity ringing in his voice. "And I wanted to see if I could help you figure out what happened to Layla."

Her eyebrows rose. "Since when do you care about the case?"

"I didn't like what you said, about me hating Layla," he admitted, suddenly looking sad. "She might have annoyed me when we were younger, but I never hated her. She was just my kid sister's pesky friend. And I really am sorry she was killed, Mor."

"I know." She ignored a stab of guilt. "I didn't mean to accuse you of hating her. You hit the nail on the head—I was lashing out."

Tony grinned. "Told you so."

She rolled her eyes. "You deserved it."

The sound of footsteps came from the hall and a moment later Quinn strode into the kitchen. Morgan immediately experienced a healthy rush of lust when she saw him. Denim encased his long legs, and the black long-sleeve shirt he wore stretched across his broad chest. His hair was wet and slicked back from his face. He hadn't shaved though. Dark stubble dotted his strong jaw, reminding Morgan of the delicious way those whiskers had scraped over her flesh.

She lowered her head before he noticed the flush on her face, but Quinn never missed a thing. His hot gaze pierced her, and when she gathered the courage to lift her head and meet his eyes, the sheer lust she saw in them made her choke on her coffee. Coughing, she set her mug down on the counter.

"You okay?" Quinn said, his voice casual.

"Yeah, it just went down the wrong tube, that's all," she lied.

Quinn smothered a laugh, knowing exactly where Morgan's train of thought had taken her. She looked flustered and un-believably cute, but she recovered quickly. As he accepted the cup Tony offered him, Morgan waited until her brother's head was turned to shoot Quinn a lazy, self-assured smile. Then she swept her tongue along her top lip and suddenly Quinn didn't feel like laughing anymore.

Awareness sizzled in his blood. He broke the eye contact before his body could respond to Morgan's sensual tease.

Leaning against the counter, he found Tony staring at him warily. He stared right back, until Tony finally offered a sheepish grin. "Sorry I acted like an ass out there, Quinn. My protective brotherly instincts kicked in."

"No harm done," Quinn answered.

"So," Tony began, tapping his fingers against the counter, "have you guys made any progress in the case?"

"No," Morgan confessed.

She quickly told him about their visit to the M.E.'s office and the autopsy report. Tony didn't seem optimistic about either. "Sounds like you have nothing," he said wearily. He paused. "Are you sure it wasn't Jake? He was the last person to see her alive."

"I know." She stuck her chin out glumly. "But I don't think it's him, Tony. Jake's a hothead, sure, but he has no motive. He and Layla had already been broken up, and if I remember correctly, neither of them seemed too upset about it."

"Maybe he was upset," Tony countered. "But just didn't show it." He glanced at Quinn. "What do you think?"

"I'm inclined to agree with your sister. I was there last night when Jake denied it, and the denial didn't trigger my bullshit alarm."

Morgan slid off the stool and picked up her coffee mug. "Quinn and I were going to look over the files again, see if anything jumps out. You could help if you'd like."

Tony nodded. "Sure."

"I'll go get them."

Morgan left the kitchen, returning a few moments later with the files. As she dropped the stack of papers on the huge cedar table on the other side of the kitchen, she shot her brother a sideways glance. "How's Caroline?"

Tony's features softened. "She's great."

They drifted over to the table, while Tony offered a few details about his new girlfriend, who apparently worked at a rival advertising agency.

"We hated each other at first," Tony said with a grin. "I thought she was trying to steal one of our clients."

"I'm glad you gave her a chance," Morgan said as she sat down. "It's nice to see you in a relationship."

"It's nice to be in one." Tony smiled again, then reached for one of the reports in the pile. "All right, should we get started?"

They pored over the files for the next hour, until Quinn's eyes started hurting from staring at the small black print. He skimmed the autopsy report again and came up with nothing. Perused the interview with Layla's parents, nothing. Read Jake's statement, nothing. And yet despite the absolute lack of clues, something bugged him about the reports. He read

Jake's interview again, then picked up the one with Layla's folks, and although the nagging feeling in the back of his brain persisted, he couldn't bring whatever it was to the forefront.

He scratched his chin. "Something's bugging me but I can't quite put my finger on it."

Morgan glanced at the file in his hand. "Layla's parents?"

He nodded.

She chewed on her bottom lip. "The last time Mort and Wendy saw their daughter was that morning, before she left for school. I talked to them, and I think they genuinely had no idea what happened."

"Yeah, but…" Quinn glanced at the paper again, just as Tony's hand reached for it.

"Mind if I take a look?" Tony asked. "I haven't read this one yet."

Quinn handed over the file and glanced back at Morgan, whose forehead was furrowed in a frown. "Why can't we find a single lead?" she said in frustration.

Quinn sighed. "Because there's nothing here. All we know is that ten years ago Layla went into the woods, either to meet someone or to go for a run, and she never came out. When she disappeared, the police searched every inch of the woods and found nothing. They talked to everyone in town, found nothing."

"He's right, there's nothing here," Tony said, setting down the report. He directed a sympathetic look in his sister's direction. "I don't think you're going to solve this case, Morgan."

She bit her lip again. "I have to. I owe it to Layla."

Neither man said anything.

Quinn finally let out a breath. "Like I said before, I think we need to focus on whoever ran you off the bridge. That trail is hotter than this one."

"Let's go to the bridge then," she announced. Her chair

scraped the tiled floor as she pushed it back, standing up in determination.

"Now?" Quinn said warily.

"Now."

She had that look in her eyes that said not even a speeding train rushing toward her could stop her from plowing ahead. Quinn glanced at Tony, who looked slightly amused.

"Now it is," Quinn said, rising from his chair.

Quinn stood a short distance from Morgan and watched as she peered down at the river in frustration. The bridge was on the other side of town, hovering over Grace River, a small body of water with a mild current. The bridge was wide, with two wooden railings on each side. Steel would have been a better choice, Quinn mused. Steel would probably have stopped Morgan's car from going over. Wood broke.

The town had rebuilt the broken rail, and as the three of them walked around, it became painfully obvious there was nothing to find. The river below was quiet, save for the soft sound of water splashing against the muddy banks.

Pausing at the railing, Quinn's jaw tensed. The water wasn't very deep, but deep enough to submerge a vehicle. He imagined Morgan's car down there, slowly sinking to the silt at the bottom of the river. Anger clawed at his gut like a hungry animal. She could have died, damn it.

"I should get going," came Tony's quiet voice.

Quinn looked up to see Tony approach, a somber expression on his face. "We're not going to find anything," Morgan's brother added, his gaze drifting over to where Morgan stood.

She was still looking down at the water, the stiffness of her shoulders revealing her dissatisfaction over not discovering any clues out here.

"You're not staying the night?" Quinn asked.

Tony shook his head. "I've got plans with Caroline tonight,

and I promised I'd be back this afternoon." He hesitated. "Look, can I be frank with you?"

Quinn nodded guardedly.

"The senator sent me," Tony admitted, keeping his voice low. "He wanted me to bring her home."

"She won't go back until she's ready."

"I know. That's why I'm not pushing. It's obvious she's not going to figure out what happened to Layla, and I think in a day or two she'll realize that and leave voluntarily."

As opposed to by force, which was what her bastard of a father wanted. Quinn suddenly stared at the man beside him, baffled. "Why are you so loyal to him?" he couldn't help but ask.

Tony didn't seem offended by the question. "He's my father," he said simply. "With Mom gone, Dad is all we've got. I see no harm in going along with him, within reason."

"And it's reasonable to have your sister committed to a psychiatric word?"

Tony flinched at the barb. "It wasn't my idea. But to be honest, I'm still not sure she didn't drive off intentionally. I was with her after the memorial, Quinn. She was devastated."

"Morgan wouldn't try to kill herself."

"I'm not sure," Tony said again. His eyes strayed to his sister once more. "Look, I don't know what's going on between you two, but you need to encourage her to quit investigating a case that's not likely to be solved. The senator is getting impatient."

"Why?" Quinn shook his head in bewilderment. "Why does he care if she investigates?"

"I don't know." Tony's voice lowered. "But he's determined to bring her home. He said he'd use extreme measures if need be."

Quinn clenched his teeth. "Send out the men in white coats?"

"Maybe." Tony sighed. "You know my father. He likes

everything in a neat and tidy package. Looking good is his main concern, and my sister, unfortunately, has the bad habit of making him look bad. He doesn't like that he's unable to control her."

"Well, he better get used to it," Quinn said with a humorless laugh. "Because Morgan isn't easily controlled."

Tony smiled ruefully. "No, she certainly isn't." He glanced at the expensive Rolex on his wrist, then said, "Think you guys can drop me back at the house now? I need to get going."

"I'll get Morgan."

Quinn walked in her direction, and quietly cleared his throat. "Morgan, we have to go."

She slowly turned away from the railing, and the disappointment and sorrow in her big blue eyes nearly tore him apart. "There's nothing here," she mumbled. "No second set of tire tracks, no paint flecks, no sign that there was another car."

"I know. That's why we need to leave." He gestured to her brother, who stood by the SUV. "And Tony wants to head back to D.C."

"All right," she said.

They drove back to the Kerr estate in silence, and Tony's goodbye was subdued. He, too, looked disappointed that they hadn't found anything. But Quinn could swear he also looked pleased. No doubt he'd go straight to the senator to deliver the good news that Morgan kept hitting a brick wall in the case and would probably be home soon. Senator Kerr would be ecstatic.

By the time evening rolled around, Morgan went from depressed to frustrated to angry, and now back to depressed. She and Quinn spent the afternoon reading the case files again, coming up with nothing—again. Eventually they decided to take a break, and ended up playing a game of Scrabble. It should have been fun—they used to play a lot when they'd been together—but not even the familiar activity could lift her spirits.

She felt like a failure. For ten years she'd come back to Autumn, asked questions, read the reports, and for ten years she'd returned to D.C. with nothing. Layla had disappeared a decade ago, last seen going into the woods, and a decade later, her body had been found. That was all they knew. All they'd ever know.

The discouraging details filled her with despair, and as much as she hated admitting it, maybe it was time to give up. She spent most of the evening going back and forth on the subject, battling her own nature. She wasn't a quitter, never had been. But how long could she keep looking under stones and find nothing but dirt underneath?

Quinn wisely said very little as she pondered. He prepared spaghetti for dinner, which they ate quietly, and then Morgan retreated to her study, where she sat for two hours, trying to figure out what to do.

In the end, she decided to do nothing. For tonight, anyway. She would go to sleep, rest her tired brain and figure it out in the morning.

Rising from her chair, she headed for the doorway, just as the phone rang. She sighed and went back to the desk. Her brother's cell number flashed on the phone's digital screen.

"You again," she said, half teasing, half sighing.

"Hey, Mor. Sorry to bug you, but I forgot to tell you something earlier. Caroline's birthday is next week, and I'm throwing a surprise party for her." He sounded almost boyish as he said, "I'd like for you to come. I think you two would get along well."

She was touched that he'd invite her. She and Tony hadn't spent much time together since their mother died. "I'd love to," she said. "Did you get back to the city okay?"

"Yep, barely any traffic. I just left Caroline's apartment and I'm heading home now."

"Drive safely," she said. "And thanks for the invite."

"I'll talk to you soon," her brother said, then hung up.

Morgan set down the phone and left the study, shutting the door behind her. At the foot of the staircase in the foyer, she hesitated. Should she go up to Quinn's room, or her own? After the constant letdowns of the day, she was aching to fall into his arms and make love to him. But she wasn't sure if he meant for last night to be a one-shot deal.

In the end, she went up to her own room. Quinn had been very supportive today, but she still had no idea where his head—and heart—was at. And the last thing she wanted to deal with right now was his rejection.

She changed into her pajamas and turned off the light, bathing the bedroom in darkness. Sliding under the covers, she shifted around until she found a comfortable position. She'd thought sleep would be hard to come by, but to her surprise, the fatigue of the day got the better of her. She was just drifting into that half-asleep, half-awake state, her muscles loose and relaxed, when a soft knock sounded on the door.

"Come in," she said sleepily.

The door opened and light spilled in from the hallway. She opened her eyes in time to glimpse Quinn's silhouette fill the narrow door frame.

"Hey," he said. "Did I wake you?"

"No, I was only kinda sleeping."

Even in the dark, she could see his green eyes gleam with amusement. "Kinda? It looks like more than kinda."

She rolled onto her side, rested her cheek on the pillow and said, "Is there something you want, Quinn?"

He sounded gruff. "Just wanted to let you know I'm going to take a shower and go to bed. I wanted to say good-night."

"All right." A tiny pang of regret tugged at her belly. So, she'd been right not to go to him. He evidently had no intention of repeating last night's passionate activities.

His Adam's apple bobbed as he swallowed. "Do you want me to come up when I'm out of the shower?"

Her heart jumped in surprise. Okay, so maybe she'd been wrong. She lifted her head off the pillow, and her breath hitched when she saw the look in his eyes. It was a cross between sweet uncertainty and sinful promise.

"Yes," she whispered in response to his question.

He turned for the door.

"You can shower here, you know," she said.

"I need to charge my phone and grab some boxers." His eyes twinkled. "Don't worry, I'll be up soon."

He shut the door carefully and the bedroom went dark again. Ribbons of happiness uncurled in her body. She released a contented sigh and let herself drift off again, longing for Quinn's return. She imagined him sliding under the warm covers, wrapping one strong arm around her. God, she'd missed sleeping with him.

The door creaked open again. It seemed too fast—hadn't he just left? She was too lethargic to open her eyes, simply murmuring, "Back so soon?"

Quinn didn't answer, but his footsteps thudded softly on the carpet as he approached the bed. Smiling, Morgan reached to pull up the covers. Instead of joining her under the blanket, he whipped it aside. The sudden loss of warmth surprised her. She blinked her eyes and found an ominous face covered by a black ski mask hovering over her.

And then a gloved hand clamped over her mouth.

Chapter 14

Panic pummeled into Morgan's chest like angry fists. She tried to scream, but the intruder's hand tightly covered her mouth, her frantic sounds muffled against the leather glove he wore. So she used her teeth instead of her voice, wildly biting the long gloved fingers but failing to dig her teeth in.

Her attacker snaked his other arm under her back and forcibly hauled her off the bed. She landed on the carpet with a thud and for a moment his hand slipped from her mouth. Hope burst inside her and she opened her mouth to scream for Quinn but Ski Mask quickly slapped his palm back into place. He didn't say a word as he dragged her across the carpet, while she kicked her legs hoping to connect with something. Fear seized her spine. She couldn't let him take her. She had to make some noise, alert Quinn.

And there was no doubt the intruder planned on taking her. She didn't know how he got into the house, why none of the alarms had gone off, but his iron-tight grasp and purposeful strides made his intentions clear.

.Adrenaline sizzled through her veins. She kept kicking, trying to bite, screaming muted sounds against the glove, but whoever this guy was, he was strong. She'd taken self-defense classes over the years, but she was no match for Ski Mask.

Or so she thought. The second he got her to the door, his hand slipped again, and this time she managed to rip out a shriek so loud she was surprised the crystal chandelier downstairs didn't shatter into a million pieces. But it got the job done. Her attacker instantly froze. Then, to her extreme shock, he let her go. Shoved her so hard she fell backward, her butt landing on the floor.

Her attacker's hurried footsteps burned tracks on the hardwood floor in the hall. She stared in shock as he sprinted off, as if he'd decided not to go through with his mission.

Dazed, she stumbled to her feet. Downstairs the front door slammed, and then absolutely nothing. No hum of an engine starting, no tires screeching on the driveway. Wherever he'd gone, Ski Mask hadn't done it by car.

Unable to comprehend what just happened, she tore down the hall toward the stairs, taking them two at a time as she raced up to the third-floor guest room. Breathing heavily, a pure dose of adrenaline still pumping through her, she threw open Quinn's door and found his room empty. The sound of running water came from the bathroom. He was in the shower. She'd nearly been *kidnapped* and her big tough mercenary was in the shower.

Her hands shook like crazy as she stormed into the bathroom. Not even the sight of Quinn's wet, naked body through the glass shower door could dispel the fear and fury churning inside her.

Quinn's eyes widened at her sudden appearance. Instantly shutting off the water, he whipped open the door of the shower stall. "What's wrong?" he demanded.

"Someone just attacked me in my room," she blurted out.

Without hesitation, Quinn stepped out of the stall and

pulled her into his arms. Water dripped from his body, soaking her pajamas, but she didn't care. As tears pricked her eyelids, she buried her face against his damp chest.

"He was wearing a ski mask...I thought it was you at first... he tried to drag me out...I..." Each sentence shot out like a bullet from a rifle. "I screamed and he took off...I didn't hear a car start. He might have run into the woods."

Quinn released her and bounded out of the washroom. She followed him into the bedroom and watched as he slid a pair of gray sweatpants over his legs. He charged toward the nightstand, grabbed his gun, then bent down by the duffel near the door and unzipped it. He retrieved another weapon, a menacing black Glock, and stuck it out in her direction, butt first. "You remember how to use this?" he asked, his tone deadly.

She nodded numbly.

"Good." He made for the door. "Lock yourself in the bathroom. Don't open the door for anyone but me."

Her eyes widened as he raced off. He was going after the attacker. Dear God, don't let him get hurt. Her instincts told her to run after him, but Quinn's orders had been nonnegotiable. With tears running down her face, she locked herself in the bathroom as he'd requested, then sank down onto the wet floor and leaned against the side of marble tub. She held the gun with both hands, keeping it aimed at the door. And then she waited.

And waited. And waited.

It was a good thirty minutes later when Quinn came back. He knocked and told her to open up, which she did immediately.

"Well?" she demanded, clutching the gun in her hands.

His chest was still damp, but now from sweat. His ragged breaths indicated he'd been doing some serious running. But the look on his face was one of puzzlement. "There's nobody here," he said.

Relief and confusion collided inside her. She followed Quinn into the bedroom, where she lowered herself on the edge of the bed, setting the gun on the mattress. "You didn't find him?"

Quinn stood in front of her, an odd flicker in his eyes. "No. In fact, I found no signs that anyone had been in the house. The front door was locked, Morgan. The alarm was armed."

A chill scurried up her spine.

"I walked the perimeter," he continued, still eyeing her with that indefinable expression. "I checked the yard, scoured the edge of the woods for tracks, circled the entire house. I couldn't find any trace of the guy."

"He's good then," she murmured.

Quinn didn't respond. His silence caused a warning bell to go off in her head, and when she lifted her head to meet his eyes, she finally deciphered the peculiar expression.

It was doubt.

He didn't believe her.

Her chest felt as if it had been crushed by a five-ton weight. "You think I'm making it up?" she said in a small voice.

Quinn's brows furrowed with indecision. "No, I don't think you're making it up. I'm leaning toward, uh, maybe a nightmare?"

Disbelief whipped around inside her like an unsecured cable in the middle of a windstorm. "A nightmare? You think I don't know the difference between a nightmare, and actually waking up to a *strange man* dragging me out of bed?"

He faltered. "It just doesn't make any sense. Why would he try to drag you off, then run away like a scared rabbit? How did he get in the house? Why is the alarm on and the front door locked?"

Morgan's cheeks scorched. She curled her fingers into fists and sent Quinn a venomous look. "I did not dream this, or imagine it." She spoke through clenched teeth. "And I can think of a very good reason how the intruder got inside. My father sent him."

She stumbled off the bed and stalked to the door. "The guy probably had a key, a code for the alarm, and I'm sure my dad told him exactly how to get off the property through the ravine."

Quinn cursed softly from behind. "He just wanted to scare you, not take you. Wanted to freak you out enough that you'd leave on your own."

"Probably." She tossed him an icy glance over her shoulder. "But then again, I could have dreamed that, too."

Without another word, she stormed out of the guest room, her heart thrashing angrily in her chest. He'd doubted her. After everything they'd shared, after all those times she'd confessed her insecurities, told him how much it hurt hearing other people accuse her of being nuts...after all that, he'd doubted her.

She'd barely reached the landing when Quinn tugged on her arm and yanked her back, forcing her to stop. "Morgan, come on. Look at me."

She childishly kept her gaze on the floor.

"Look at me," he repeated firmly. When she still refused, he cupped her chin with both hands and forced the eye contact.

"You didn't believe me," she muttered, unable to stop the pain that seeped into her tone.

"I'm sorry." His green eyes glittered with remorse. "But you've got to see it from my point of view. I was in the shower, so I didn't hear a thing, and I just spent the last half hour combing the woods for a phantom. It made no sense."

"So you just assume I imagined it all?" she said sardonically.

He released her chin, but didn't let her go. His hands

merely drifted down to her waist. "I'm sorry. It wasn't until you mentioned your father that I remembered…extreme measures," he said quietly.

"Huh?"

"Tony said those words earlier. Don't get angry, but he admitted your father sent him here to bring you home—"

"I knew it!"

"—and that the senator was willing to take extreme measures to get you back." Quinn gave a cynical smile. "I guess this is his idea of extreme."

Sadness settled in her belly. What kind of man would do that to his own daughter? Morgan always knew her dad was selfish, but this went beyond selfish. He'd *committed* her. He'd probably just sent some goon to scare the wits out of her. Who did that?

And why?

"Why?" She voiced the troubling thought aloud. "Why does he want me home so badly? Who am I hurting by looking into Layla's death?"

"Him, indirectly, anyway." Quinn gently ran his fingers along her hips, his touch soothing. "Last time you came to investigate you ended up leaving in an ambulance, which of course ended up in the papers. We both know he doesn't like any negative attention directed at him, sweetheart."

"Well, screw him," she mumbled. Her eyes started to sting. "I've spent my entire life trying to please him. I did it for my mom. I'm *still* doing it for her. I promised her I'd support him no matter what." She shook her head bitterly. "Hell, I gave up the man I love for him. You'd think that would be an acceptable show of support."

Quinn's face hardened, making her regret the callous words. But it was true. She'd made a promise to her mother, and she'd kept the promise, no matter how many times she'd been tempted to tell her father to screw off. The senator had never even thanked her.

"I don't think you should have ever forgiven me," she whispered, slanting her head to look into his eyes. "I don't deserve it. I chose him over you, when deep down I knew it was the wrong thing." Bile nearly gagged her. "I threw you away like a piece of garbage."

Quinn seemed a little shell-shocked. His pulse vibrated in his throat, and she could feel his fingers trembling against her pelvic bone. "It's in the past," he muttered. "Forget it."

She pushed his hands off of her, tears filling her eyes. "I can't forget it. And I can't do this anymore, dig around in the past. I'm done investigating, Quinn. At this point, I don't give a damn who killed Layla."

Quinn's face revealed that he knew she didn't mean what she said, that she *did* care. "Don't give up," he said huskily, his green eyes imploring.

A tear slid down her cheek. He brushed it away with his thumb, his touch infinitely gentle and unbelievably warm. His lips were equally gentle as he dipped his head and kissed her. He swept his tongue into her mouth. She tasted the saltiness of her tears, mingled with the familiar flavor of Quinn, hot and masculine and utterly delicious.

They stood in the hallway for what seemed like hours, while Quinn's mouth brushed over hers in feather-light kisses that drained the anxiety from her body and left her feeling warm and gooey and weightless.

When he finally broke the kiss, his eyes shone with tenderness and encouragement. "We'll take one more look at the files tomorrow, okay?"

"Okay," she agreed.

"Good." He stroked her cheek for a moment, then took a step back and held out his hand. "Shall we go to bed?"

A multitude of emotions swirled inside her. She stared into his sexy green eyes, then his outstretched hand, and the emotions rippled and danced until they became one concrete thread of love that wrapped around her heart.

Never taking his eyes off him, she placed her hand in his and said, "Yes."

As she'd promised, Morgan gave the case files another go the next morning. She and Quinn woke up early, and after a quick breakfast featuring Quinn's mouthwatering cheese omelets, they set a pot of coffee in the middle of the kitchen table and got to work. Twenty minutes later, Morgan had officially given up. Quinn was still studying the files, but she'd read them so many times her eyes were starting to cross, and at this point, she couldn't fathom finding anything new from the bare details she already had. She was now doing the crossword puzzle in Autumn's daily newspaper, pleased to find the editors had decided to branch away from clues like *feline* for three letters, and dish out some more challenging clues.

"I need a synonym for deportation, eight letters," she said.

"Break-ins," Quinn mumbled.

Morgan glanced down at the puzzle and frowned. "Huh? That doesn't make sense. I think it might be eviction, but that would mean six down is wrong because it doesn't have a *v*. Are you sure—"

"I'm not talking about the puzzle," he interrupted. "I figured out what's bothering me." Looking victorious, he held up the report he was reading. "The follow-up interview with Layla's parents. It says that a few days after her disappearance, there were several break-ins on the Simmses' street."

She put down the newspaper, frowning again. "Yeah, so?"

"So you didn't find it odd that Layla's house was broken into five days after she disappeared?"

"Of course I did," she retorted, bristling at the implication that she hadn't thoroughly scrutinized the matter. "I did some investigating, and couldn't find a connection between the two. Six houses on the street were hit. Mostly jewelry and cash was taken, and I talked to all the victims."

"Did the burglar take anything from the Simmses' house?"

She nodded. "Some jewelry that belonged to Wendy Simms, and a couple of rings from Layla's room."

Quinn leaned back in the chair and rubbed absently at his unshaven chin. "Was Layla's house robbed first?"

"No, I think it might have been the fourth. The sheriff at the time suspected it was some misfit from my high school, taking advantage of the fact that the police were focusing on Layla's vanishing act and thus not paying attention to the rest of the town." She smiled faintly. "I think Grady Parker might have been brought in for questioning."

"What if it wasn't a burglar?" Quinn said suddenly. "What if the break-ins were nothing but a red herring? What if the killer—"

"Wanted something of Layla's?" she interjected. She let out a sigh. "Yeah, I thought of that, too. Layla had something that might incriminate her killer, so he or she broke in to a bunch of houses, but really only cared about one house in particular. He or she searched her room, probably found the item and tied up the loose ends."

"What if he didn't find it?" Quinn countered. His eyes were suddenly animated. "What if Layla did have something incriminating, and it's still in that house? Did you ever search her room?"

"No," Morgan admitted. "By the time I'd seriously started investigating, Layla's parents had gotten rid of most of her things and turned her bedroom into an office. There were some boxes in the attic, which I went through, but I didn't find anything."

"But what about the room itself?" he asked. "Did you ever search it?"

"No." She shot him a thoughtful look. "You think we should."

"Yeah. I have a good feeling about this. I think the break-ins are connected to this case, and my instincts are telling me Layla had something that belonged to her killer, or, in the very least, something that could lead us to him."

"Unless he found it," she said again.

Quinn shook his head. "I don't think he did. Someone tried to kill you, which means there must be some piece of evidence lying around that could lead to the killer. If he'd gotten what he wanted during the robberies, he wouldn't be worried." He gestured to the files. "There are absolutely no clues in here, sweetheart. Whoever killed her has to know that. So there's no reason for them to worry about getting caught."

"Unless there's still one clue that could expose them," she concluded.

"I think Layla knew her killer," Quinn said slowly. "And knew him well. Are you sure she wasn't seeing anyone?"

"No one she told me about."

"But she was meeting someone in the woods. And considering the turbulent emotions that must have been present in order for him to kill her in such a brutal fashion, I think she was involved with the killer."

Morgan's brain worked hard to keep up with the stream of information coming in. Every word Quinn said made sense, and it was all details she'd considered before. It had never made sense that Layla was killed by a random stranger. Autumn wasn't the kind of town that attracted many sadistic killers. The occasional drunk tourist, sure, but it hadn't felt right, the notion that someone had passed through town, killed Layla and then went on their merry way.

Layla had known her killer, and like Quinn, Morgan's instincts suddenly started to hum. She'd always suspected the break-ins were related, but it wasn't a lead she'd pursued vigorously. Now, she felt confident that Layla's bedroom might hold the key to solving this case.

Her chair scraped the floor as she pushed it back. "Let's go now. Mr. Simms is probably at work, but Wendy should be home."

Energy sizzled in the air as they drove to Layla's house, which was about a ten-minute drive from the Kerr estate. They didn't say much, but the silence didn't bother her. She suddenly felt keyed up, excited even. Maybe they would only be in for another disappointment, but this was the first time in years that a clue had materialized, and Morgan prayed it wouldn't be another dead end.

Layla's house was a large bungalow with pretty green shutters and an even prettier garden. Despite the fact that it was late October, Mrs. Simms's begonias were as vibrant as ever, bringing a splash of color to the otherwise dull front lawn. The Simmses owned the only greenhouse and flower shop in town, and Wendy Simms often took on private land-scaping projects when it suited her. Today, fortunately, she was at home, which Morgan deduced when she spotted the ancient beige station wagon in the driveway. Wendy had been driving that station wagon since Morgan was in diapers. It was a miracle the thing still ran.

She and Quinn walked up the narrow cobblestone path to the front door, where she rang the bell. Anticipation coiled inside her at the prospect of finally—hopefully—getting somewhere with this case.

The door swung open to reveal Wendy Simms, a short, dark-haired woman in her late fifties. She wore a checkered apron, had a smudge of flour on her cheeks and a smile on her face when she saw Morgan.

"Oh, honey, it's so good to see you!" she chirped, immediately pulling Morgan in for a tight, warm hug. "How are you feeling? I was so worried when I heard about the accident."

Wendy was the first person in town who actually said the word *accident* as if she *meant* the word *accident*. Morgan experienced a rush of love and gratitude. She'd always adored Layla's mom.

"I'm doing okay," she reassured the older woman. After an awkward beat, she gestured to Quinn. "This is Quinn, a friend of mine. Can we come in?"

"Of course."

Wendy ushered them inside and spent a few moments fussing over Morgan like a mother hen. She decided that Morgan was too thin, too pale and shouldn't have left the hospital so soon.

If she knew which ward of the hospital Morgan had been in, she'd probably alter that opinion.

When Wendy finally stopped to take a breath, Morgan explained why they were there. A shadow immediately fell over the other woman's face, making Morgan feel like a total heel for coming. But Wendy didn't seem upset about the visit, just the circumstances leading to it.

"I don't understand what Sheriff Wilkinson is doing over there in the station," Wendy muttered, her brown eyes flashing with resentment. "Sometimes I think you're the only one, aside from Mort and me, who cares that my daughter was murdered."

Morgan completely understood the anger she saw on Wendy's face. God knew she'd felt it plenty of times during the past ten years.

"I don't think you'll find anything in her room," Wendy confessed, looking disappointed, as if their search had already resulted in nothing. "But you're welcome to go up and look."

"Thanks, Mrs. Simms," she said gratefully. "Would you like to come up with us?"

Layla's mother shook her head. She averted her eyes, but not before Morgan glimpsed the spark of pain in them. "You go ahead, Morgan. I've got some dough waiting for me in the kitchen. I'm making biscuits for dinner tonight."

As Mrs. Simms drifted off in the direction of the kitchen, Quinn glanced at Morgan. "She's a sweet lady," he said in a low voice.

"Definitely." Her gaze darkened. "She didn't deserve what happened to her and her family. Come on, Layla's room is at the end of the hall."

She led Quinn down the corridor leading toward the bedrooms. Layla had often complained about how much she hated living in a bungalow. Her room was directly across from her parents', and the two girls had been admonished to be quiet dozens of times whenever Morgan slept over.

She opened the door, a little disoriented to see the neat office her friend's bedroom had been transformed into. A long, cedar desk rested against one wall, right where Layla's bed used to sit, and the two metal file cabinets had once been Layla's bookshelves. She'd been an avid reader.

"Where do we start?" Morgan asked, looking at Quinn.

"The floor."

She raised a brow.

"You already went through her things," he elaborated. "Which means if she hid anything, it's in the floor, or the walls, or the closet."

"The floor it is," she said cheerfully.

She felt slightly silly as she got down on her knees and began running her hands along the hardwood floor. She knocked on it, poked at it, pried it with her fingers hoping to find a loose board. Across the room, Quinn did the same. He even moved the desk aside, effortlessly, despite its obvious mass. He tapped on the floor underneath, looked at Morgan and shook his head.

"Walls?" she said with a sigh.

Again they started at opposite sides of the room, knocking

away on the smooth white walls, hoping to find a hollow spot. Again, they found nothing.

Meeting in the middle of the room, the two of them swiveled their heads in the direction of the small closet.

"Our last hope," Morgan murmured, slowly heading for the plain white door.

She opened it, then stepped inside the cramped space. She checked the walls first, hoping to discover an indication that something lay behind them. Once more to no avail. But when she examined the floorboards, something caught her eye. The boards in the corner seemed uneven. She scooted over and dug her fingernail under the side of one board, gently prying it open. It lifted easily and something metallic glinted up from the gaping hole.

"I found something," she burst out.

"What is it?"

"Hold on a sec..." She stuck her hand inside and rummaged until her fingers connected with a solid object. A box. A thrill shot through her as she extracted the box from its hiding place.

She jumped to her feet and held it up for Quinn to see. The box was the size of a paperback novel, a thin metal rectangle with a rusty lid, no lock. And it had been sitting under the floor for a decade, perhaps containing the key to Layla's death.

"Open it," Quinn said, looking amused by her motionless state.

Morgan's heart pounded as she lifted the lid and peeked at the contents of the little box. A few snapshots of Layla and Jake rested at the top. She pulled them out and kept looking, finding a couple hundred dollars in small bills, most likely Layla's tips from Jessie's Restaurant, where she'd worked during the summers. Under the money were a couple movie ticket stubs, some birthday cards, a silly "friend of the year" pin Morgan had given her in freshman year. She moved the objects aside, lifted one of the greeting cards and noticed another item.

And then all the color drained from her face.

Shock stung her cheeks like a slap to the face, and suddenly her lungs seemed incapable of drawing in oxygen. "Oh my God," she whispered.

Chapter 15

Quinn instantly knew something was wrong. Morgan's face was devoid of color, and the sheer devastation lining her beautiful features told him she'd just seen something cataclysmic. The box shook in her hands, so violently that he felt compelled to take it from her.

Unable to fight the curiosity, he searched the tin until he spotted what he suspected spurred the horrified reaction from Morgan. It was a gorgeous ruby pendant hanging from a thin silver chain. The vivid red stone was nestled in a pear-shaped setting, surrounded by a cluster of sparkling diamonds. It looked disgustingly expensive and completely out of place with the rest of the knickknacks in the box.

"I take it you recognize this," Quinn said softly, holding up the necklace by its clasp. The ruby and diamonds glittered in the thin patch of sunlight coming in from the open curtains.

Morgan stared at him in anguish. "It belonged to my mother."

Oh, boy. A hundred different thoughts—most of them of

the disturbing variety—swamped his brain, but he forced himself not to speak any of them aloud. Instead, he focused on the one possibility that didn't seem as appalling. "Is there any chance she could have stolen it?"

Morgan shook her head, her expression dull. "No. All of Mom's jewelry is locked up in the safe in my dad's study. I don't even know the combination."

He searched her face carefully. "Who does?"

"Only my father."

Those three words sent an icy chill up Quinn's back. Yep, that's what he'd been afraid of.

"What about Tony?" he inquired.

"Only my father," she repeated, her voice lined with dismay, and a twinge of disbelief.

A short silence fell over the room. Quinn had no clue what to say. In all honesty, he hadn't seen this coming. Senator Kerr was a first-class ass, sure, but a killer? Quinn would have bet on Jake, or hell, even a random tourist, before placing a wager on Edward Kerr.

"He gave this to her," Morgan whispered. "There is no other way she could have this pendant, Quinn. My...*father* must have given it to her."

Her blue eyes conveyed a swarm of emotions. Horror and shock. Rage and betrayal. Confusion. Pain. He knew exactly what she was thinking—why would Senator Kerr kill Layla? *Had* he done it?

"Let's get out of here," Quinn announced. He snapped the box's lid shut, tucked it under his arm and reached for Morgan's hand.

Before they left the Simmses' house, they ducked into the kitchen to thank Wendy for letting them poke around, but neither of them said a word about the box they found, which Quinn had slipped into the pocket of his jacket. There was no point in upsetting Wendy or raising her suspicions, when they didn't have proof that the senator killed her daughter. The necklace hinted at his possible guilt, but until they knew for sure, they would keep it to themselves.

In the car, Morgan's hands shook wildly as she buckled her seat belt. Quinn reversed out of the driveway and peeled away from the house. It wasn't until they were halfway back to the Kerr estate that he spoke again.

"It might not be him," he said, attempting to inject some reassurance to his voice.

Morgan did not look reassured. "Nobody knows the combination of my father's safe except him. He gave her that pendant." Her voice wavered. "Do you think he was seeing her?"

"I honestly don't know."

Revulsion lined her face. "She was seventeen years old when she died. He was forty-three. Oh, God, if he was sleeping with her…" She trailed off, the disgust in her tone revealing precisely how she felt about *that* idea.

Quinn took one hand off the wheel and placed it over Morgan's. "We don't know if he was involved," he reiterated. "Layla could've gotten her hands on the necklace a hundred different ways."

Morgan's icy fingers gripped his palm. "What do you think?" she asked.

He kept his gaze on the road.

"Quinn," she persisted.

Drawing in his breath, he shot her a sideways look. "I think someone gave her the necklace."

"My father?"

He released the breath. "Probably."

"Oh, God."

They reached the front gates and Quinn rolled down the window so he could punch the code into the keypad. The gates parted to let the car drive through. He parked by a stone statue of a naked cherub holding a lute, and killed the engine. When he reached for the door handle, Morgan murmured, "No, let's stay out here for a while. I can't go in there right now."

Her gaze drifted over to the mansion, fixing on the impressive second-floor veranda supported by the marble pillars below. She frowned as she looked at the house she'd grown up in, as if suddenly questioning whether the man who owned it deserved such splendor. Quinn noticed her face was still very pale, her hand still a block of ice beneath his. He rubbed his palm over her knuckles, trying to warm her up.

"It makes so much sense," she finally said, turning to meet his eyes. "Every time I've come back here over the past ten years, my father has balked. He would tell me what a waste of time it was, that there was nothing to investigate." She shivered. "But that wasn't true, was it? He just didn't want me to figure out the truth."

"What do you think happened?" Quinn asked, gently stroking her hand.

"He must have been sleeping with her," Morgan choked out. "Or trying to." She tilted her head, anger filing her eyes. "Maybe that's what happened, he tried to seduce her and she told him she wasn't interested. You know my dad, he's livid when he doesn't get his way."

Quinn experienced a niggling sense of doubt. "She rejected him so he got pissed and killed her? I don't know, sweetheart, that doesn't sound like your father. He defines the phrase 'cool as a cucumber.'"

Morgan made a discouraged sound in the back of her throat. "I know. But what other explanation is there?"

Something dawned on him, and Quinn suddenly clenched his fists. "You realize if your father is guilty of killing Layla, then he's the one who arranged your accident on the bridge."

She gasped, then gave a tiny groan of distress. "How is

that possible? I honestly can't see him trying to kill his own daughter."

"Me neither," Quinn confessed.

"But last night's intruder," she reminded him. "I still think my dad had something to do with that."

A frustrated silence descended. Quinn still couldn't wrap his brain around any of this. Senator Kerr had killed Layla? Tried to kill his daughter? Covered up a murder for ten years? On one hand, it explained a lot—Kerr's determination to keep his daughter from solving the case, his insistence that she not visit Autumn too frequently, his often irrational desire to keep Morgan securely under his thumb.

On the other hand, Quinn couldn't imagine a man as controlled and ice-cold as Edward Kerr picking up a rock and bashing in a seventeen-year-old girl's head, no matter how angry he may have been.

Morgan's soft sniffle caused Quinn to glance over at the passenger seat. When he noticed the tears streaming down her cheeks, he didn't hesitate in unbuckling her seat belt and lifting her onto his lap. Wrapping his arms around her, he ran his hand through her soft blond hair as she pressed her face to his chest and cried softly.

"What if he actually *killed* her?" she said between sobs. "What do I do? Call the police? Turn my own father in?" She buried her face in his neck, her tears soaking his skin. "God, as much as I might hate him sometimes, I don't know if I could send him to jail."

"Before you do anything drastic, I think we should go back to the city and talk to him," Quinn suggested.

She lifted her head and swiped at the moisture on her cheeks with the sleeve of her sweater. "He'll deny it," she said cynically.

"Or he might tell the truth."

Morgan rubbed her eyes, then slid her fingers higher and rubbed her temples as if she had a monstrous migraine. "I can't," she burst out. "I can't talk to him, I can't look at him. Not right now. Not tonight."

"The sooner we speak to him, the sooner we'll know if—"

"If my father is a murderer?" she interrupted angrily. "If my father hired someone to push my car over a bridge?" Her entire face abruptly collapsed. "God, Quinn, I don't think I even want to know the answers."

He touched her cheek and brushed away the new batch of tears. "You do want to know," he corrected. "You *need* to know."

"Not yet," she repeated. "I *can't* do this now."

"Morgan—"

"Please, I don't want to think about this anymore. I don't want to think about anything." Her anguished voice brought an ache to his chest. "Please make me forget."

There was no way he could ever deny her, not now, not after the shocking discovery they'd made. He lifted her chin with his thumb and brought her mouth to his, kissing her long and deep. He swallowed her anxiety and grief, wishing he could take it all into himself and spare her the turmoil he tasted on her lips. The air in the car grew thick, sizzling with urgency and desperation. It wasn't long before they'd removed their coats, before his hands were sliding underneath her sweater so he could squeeze her breasts over her bra.

Whimpering, Morgan fumbled with the button of her slacks and tugged the material down her legs.

The heat of her sex pressing against his thigh made his pulse race and his groin harden. He unzipped his jeans and released his throbbing erection. Groaning, he cupped her, rubbed her femininity for a moment, before pushing aside the crotch of her skimpy panties and teasing her opening with his tip. Morgan moaned, then put an end to any possibility of foreplay by impaling herself on his thick length.

Quinn groaned again. His fingers trembled as he held on to

her slender hips and guided her along his shaft. Their hurried breathing steamed up the SUV's windows. An inferno of need heated the small space, spiking the temperature inside the car and inside Quinn's aching body.

Morgan rode him furiously, her eyelids closing as she squeezed herself over his hard member and took all the pleasure she could get. He wasn't complaining. Her wild movements drove him wild. Her sweet feminine scent flooded his senses, and the tight sheath of her body teased him, welcomed him. Pleasure began gathering in his groin, growing, building, threatening to consume him.

"Morgan," he said between gritted teeth, "you've got to come. *Now.*"

He didn't know if she'd been close, or if his rough desperate plea pushed her over the edge, but she suddenly let out a wild cry and shuddered over him. Her release spurred his, a mind-blowing climax that seared every nerve ending and sent his mind spinning into oblivion.

It took a moment for him to crash back down to earth, and when he did, he almost laughed at what just happened. They'd had sex in the front seat of his car in the middle of the afternoon like a couple of horny teenagers. His pulse continued to race, his erection still rock-hard and buried inside of Morgan. The sight of her took his breath away. With her face flushed and her eyes heavy-lidded with passion, she was heartbreakingly beautiful.

She caught her bottom lip with her teeth, looking at him with uncertainty. And then she spoke, and her words officially drained his lungs of any remaining oxygen.

"I love you."

Quinn swallowed. "Morgan—"

"No, I need to say this. I love you, Quinn. I never stopped loving you."

The fact that their bodies were still intimately joined made it very difficult to concentrate. After a moment of reluctance, he withdrew from her warmth and zipped up his pants. Morgan pulled up her slacks and buttoned them, but her expression said "just because we're dressed doesn't mean I'm done talking."

"Say something," she said, her firm tone matching the look in her eyes.

He shifted awkwardly. "What do you want me to say?"

Instantly he regretted the question. Hell, he knew exactly what she wanted him to say. Yet he couldn't bring himself to say those same three words back to her, no matter how loudly his heart yelled for him to do it. He couldn't go down that path again. Last time he'd done it, he wound up burned and broken. This time, he planned on walking away unscathed.

"I know you still love me," she whispered, holding his gaze hostage by placing both hands on his jaw and forcing him to look at her. "And you already admitted you've forgiven me." Her voice trembled. "All you have to do now is agree to give us another chance."

"I...I can't."

He could see her biting the inside of her cheek, trying not to cry. "I'm sorry I chose him over you," she finally blurted out. Her hands dropped from his face. "I was wrong. I was wrong to let him interfere in our life, and I was wrong to let him talk me into postponing the wedding. I've always known I made the wrong choice, but I convinced myself I needed to keep the promise I made to my mom. Now I know better. I loved my mother, but my father is not the man she thought he was."

"Morgan—"

She went on, oblivious to his interjection. "It's very likely he killed my best friend, and I refuse to protect or support him any longer. I'm through with him, Quinn. I promise you, I will never put you second again."

A vise of pain circled his heart and squeezed it so tightly he feared it would splinter. Lord, how he'd longed to hear those words...two years ago.

"I know you mean that," he said gruffly. "I even believe you. But—"

"No buts." Her big blue eyes pleaded with him, ripping another hole in his heart. "Please, just give us another chance."

Very gently, he lifted her off his lap and settled her on the passenger seat. "I can't."

"Why not?" she whispered.

"Our breakup made me see I'm not cut out for relationships. I'll always demand too much of you. I'll always want my own way." He gave a wry smile. "And I don't think I could settle down in one place. I tried so freaking hard to stay put when we were together, but I realized these past two years that I like the traveling."

"Then I'll travel with you," she said softly. "I'm sick to death of D.C., Quinn. I already told you I'd like to take on more exciting assignments."

Although the idea of traveling with Morgan was appealing, he forced himself to push it aside. "I can't be with you, Morgan." It took all of his willpower to say the words. "I can't offer you the kind of relationship you deserve."

Disappointment flashed in her eyes. "You've always given me everything I've ever needed," she insisted.

He let out a sigh. "I can't argue about this anymore. When you came to my room that night, you promised you wouldn't ask for anything more." He met her eyes. "I need you to keep that promise."

She didn't say anything for a moment. Then her eyes flashed again, this time with resentment. "Fine. If you're determined to be a coward, then I won't stop you." She yanked on the door handle and swung her legs over the seat. "I'm going inside to get my purse and lock up the house."

"Morgan—"

She hopped onto the pavement. Stood in front of the passenger door, her face grim. "And I changed my mind. I want to go back to the city as soon as possible. I'll call my father from inside and tell him we're on our way. Oh, and once we've talked to my father, we'll both go our separate ways." Bitterness dripped from her voice. "So you don't have to worry. This time I'll stay out of your life for good."

Without another word, she slammed the door and walked away.

Chapter 16

The drive back to the city was somber. And silent. Deathly silent. Morgan kept her gaze glued to the window for most of the time, unable to look at Quinn for fear she'd burst into tears.

He'd rejected her.

She'd handed him her heart, and he'd handed it right back.

And the screwed-up part was that she didn't even blame him. He was right. She'd put him second so many times during their relationship. She'd let her father dictate certain aspects of their life. She'd postponed their wedding. What else could she expect from him now? Quinn had been burned and betrayed so many times during his childhood, he shouldn't have had to deal with that from his own fiancée.

God, she was a fool. She'd allowed a misguided sense of loyalty to steer her in the wrong direction. She'd lost Quinn.

And she had nobody to blame but herself.

They slowed on Constitution Avenue, just north of the

Capitol, and her chest tightened when the senate office building came into view. Made of limestone and gray granite, with elegant columns lining the entrance, the building was old and beautiful, an architectural triumph that spoke of history, wealth and justice.

Justice. The word stayed suspended in her mind, the irony of it making her want to laugh. What did the man who kept an office in this building know about justice?

Quinn parked the car, and a few minutes later they were in the building and on their way to her father's office. The door stood open, and the senator was behind his desk when she and Quinn walked into the room without an invitation. Her dad had obviously been waiting for them. The wrinkles around his mouth were creased with impatience and his blue eyes held a hint of unease.

"Hi, Dad," she said in a frosty tone.

"Morgan," he returned, equally chilly. He glowered at Quinn. "Adam."

Neither she nor Quinn sat down. She simply stood in front of her father's enormous desk, while Quinn drifted toward one of the tall bookcases and leaned against it.

"What is all this about?" Edward finally demanded, losing some of his cool.

He leaned back in his chair, attempting to look unperturbed, but she saw through the act. She knew her father well, and right now, he was worried. He knew this was an ambush and she could practically see his brain kicking into overdrive, formulating a defense to anything she might pitch at it.

"Quinn and I had a visitor last night," she began.

"If you're referring to your brother, yes, I know. I sent him," her father replied pleasantly.

"Actually, I'm referring to the masked intruder who dragged me out of bed." She glowered at him. "Who was he, Dad? A random stranger you paid off the street, or was it a professional?"

Her father's face remained blank. "I have no idea what you're talking about."

"Oh, really?" She shook her head. "You told Tony you'd use extreme methods to bring me home. I assume trying to scare the hell out of me was part of the plan."

"There is no plan." The senator frowned. "Your paranoia is acting up, Morgan. I merely wanted you home because I believe you're a danger to yourself."

She snorted. "Save the suicide story for the press. I didn't try to kill myself."

Edward sighed. "Why are you here, Morgan? You call me, order me not to leave this office until you get here because you have something important to discuss, and so far, all I'm hearing is the same old paranoid denials."

"You want something new? Fine. Quinn and I found something in Autumn."

She waited for his reaction, but her father's eyes became shuttered. "Oh?" was all he said.

Slowly, she reached into the pocket of her coat and extracted the silver pendant. She held it up.

This time he let a brief reaction slip. His eyes widened slightly at the sight of the sparking gems, but he recovered quickly, pasting on a suspicious look instead.

"That belonged to your mother. Where did you get it?"

"I found it in Layla's room. Hidden in a box under the floorboards."

"That's impossible. All of your mother's jewelry has been locked up in the safe since she died."

"Obviously not." Morgan scowled at him. "Now why would my best friend have my mother's necklace, Dad?"

"She must have stolen it," her father replied stiffly.

"Or you gave it to her," Quinn interjected, his voice utterly calm.

Morgan was having a tougher time controlling her anger. Her father looked so smug and indignant sitting there behind his fancy desk, feigning innocence about how the necklace ended up in Layla's possession.

The senator turned his attention to Quinn. "Precisely what are you implying?" he asked in a voice that could freeze the Pacific Ocean. "That I gave an underage girl an expensive piece of jewelry that belonged to my late wife? That I was involved in her death?"

"You tell us," Quinn answered.

Kerr's eyes flashed. "Neither of those is true. I don't know what wild-goose chase my daughter has sent you on, Adam, but you're an intelligent man. What motive could I possibly have for killing my daughter's friend?"

"*Your daughter* is standing right here," Morgan snapped, suddenly livid. "And I'd appreciate it if you'd quit acting like I'm not in the room." She clenched her fists, pressing them to her side. "What did you do to Layla, Dad?"

Her father's gaze slid back to her. "I did not harm a hair on that girl's head, and *I'd* appreciate it, young lady, if you didn't accuse me of crimes I did not commit."

She took a step forward and slammed the necklace on the desk. "How did she get this, Dad?"

His voice stayed even. "I don't know."

"What happened in the woods that day?"

"For God's sake, Morgan—"

"Did you get angry at her? Was she going to tell everyone about your affair? Or perhaps she was trying to end it, and you didn't like that so—"

"Stop right this instant!" The senator's eyes blazed with fury. "I did not kill that girl, you hear me? And if you don't drop this right now, Morgan, I will drag you right back to the psychiatric ward and have you put on medication."

Morgan's entire body began to shake. She'd expected a denial from him, but threats? Rage spiraled inside her, pricking at her insides like a hundred little knives. From the corner of her eye, she saw Quinn, still leaning against the bookshelf. He didn't say a word, didn't come to her rescue, and when she glanced over, she noticed a peculiar look in his eyes. He seemed puzzled, thoughtful, but she was too furious to question where his head was at right now.

She glared at her father. "Don't you dare threaten me. I am not crazy. I know it, and *you* know it, and if you try to have me committed again, I swear I will go to the media and do everything I possibly can to destroy your precious image."

Her father shook his head angrily. "This has got to stop, Morgan."

"Just look me in the eye and tell me you didn't have anything to do with Layla's death."

He frowned. "I didn't—"

"Look me in the eye," she snapped.

Slowly he lifted his head and locked his gaze to hers. He said nothing.

"Did you have anything to do with Layla's death?" she repeated, each word coming out as sharp as a needle.

"No, I did not."

Although his gaze never wavered, Morgan suddenly felt as if the floor beneath her feet was about to collapse. She'd seen it. Practically imperceptible, but she'd become a master at studying her father's expressions. And it was there.

The tiniest flicker of guilt.

"Oh, God," she whispered, swallowing back a wave of utter sickness. "You're lying. Damn it, Dad, what the hell did you do?"

Wrath lit up his eyes. With an uncharacteristic curse, he slammed both hands on the desktop, then stumbled to his feet. "Enough!" A shaky wrinkled hand reached for the telephone. "I'm calling the hospital and—"

"Don't bother," she interrupted, edging away from the desk as nausea continued to wreak havoc on her stomach. "I'm leaving."

"Like hell you are," her father snapped.

"Don't worry, I'm not going to the press," she said, acid dripping from her tone. "I won't tar and feather you. Not tonight anyway. I just can't stand the sight of you right now."

"Morgan—"

"Hang up the phone, Dad, or I call every contact I have and tell them that my father, Senator Edward Kerr, killed a teenage girl ten years ago."

She headed for the door. Quinn left his spot by the bookcase and joined her, and she almost jumped at the sound of his footsteps. He'd barely said a word during this entire confrontation, she'd almost forgotten he was here.

"Don't you dare walk out that door, Morgan," her father thundered from across the room.

"Try and stop me," she shot back before crossing the threshold. She slammed the door behind her and sagged against the wall, gasping for air.

"Hey, breathe now," Quinn urged quietly. But he didn't try and touch her. After their discussion in the car, it had become painfully obvious that their affair was over and done with.

"He's guilty," she whispered after she steadied her breathing.

Quinn chewed the inside of his cheek. "I'm not sure."

"I saw it in his eyes. He's lying, Quinn. He knows what happened to her."

"Perhaps. But I'm not convinced he's the one who killed her."

Morgan blinked back tears. "Honestly, I'm not sure it matters. Either way, I'm through with him."

Quinn didn't answer.

"I'm serious," she insisted. "I can't deal with his crap anymore. All he's ever cared about is himself, and I'm done trying to be the good daughter. Screw him." A wave of anger swelled inside her. "And you know what, Quinn? Screw you, too."

He seemed taken aback. "Where the hell did that come from?" he demanded.

"You said you forgave me, but that's not true," she shot back. "If you did, you wouldn't be so against the idea of getting back together. So it's over, okay? I've apologized, I've told you how much I love you, but I can't undo the past, and if you're not willing to give us a future with a clean slate, then there's no point in trying."

She brushed past him, but he grabbed her arm. "Where are you going?"

"My apartment," she said tersely. "And don't offer to drive me home. I'll take a cab."

His green eyes flickered with alarm. "You shouldn't be alone."

"Why not?" A lump lodged in her throat. "I've been alone for the past two years. Thanks for your help in Autumn, but you're right, it's time to go our separate ways."

"What about your father, the case?"

"Tomorrow I'll call Jake and tell him about the necklace." She gave a sour smile. "But we both know the investigation will turn up nothing. If my father killed Layla, he'll never be punished for it. But I know the truth, and I'll never forget it. Now please let go of my arm."

Reluctantly, Quinn released her, still looking uncertain. "I don't think you should go."

She looked him square in the eye and asked, "Do you love me, Quinn? Do you want to be with me?"

He hesitated.

It was all she needed.

"That's what I thought," she muttered. "Goodbye, Quinn."

Quinn stared at Morgan's retreating back. With her shoulders straight and head held high, she looked like a warrior leaving a battlefield, defeated, yet still able to take the loss with honor and dignity. He wanted to rush after her, but he forced himself to stay put.

He loved her. He was surprised she'd even asked, considering half the time he felt as if his feelings were written across his face in permanent marker. But love wasn't enough. He'd loved both his parents, and they'd thrown him away like a piece of trash. As much as he cared about Morgan, he cared about self-preservation more. He'd opened his heart to her once, and look what happened.

He couldn't do it again.

He was better off alone, anyway. Leave town, that's what he needed to do. He'd call Murphy, fly off to another hot zone and go back to work.

But he couldn't leave until he made sure Morgan was safe, which was the driving force behind his decision to walk back into Edward Kerr's office.

The senator, still behind his desk, frowned when Quinn entered the room. "What now?" Kerr demanded.

Crossing his arms over his chest, Quinn stood in front of Morgan's father, with the same expression of distaste he'd sported only days ago when he was summoned out of the blue. "I need you to promise me something."

Kerr snorted. "Don't count on it."

"Promise to leave Morgan alone," he said, ignoring the sarcasm. "You can't have her committed again."

"I can do whatever the hell I want. I'm her father."

"Sending her to a hospital won't shut her up." Quinn offered a cheerless smile. "Besides, if I find out you sent her back, I'll spill the story myself. I'm a lot harder to shut up, senator."

"I didn't kill that girl," Kerr said between clenched teeth.

Quinn studied the older man's face. "You know, I think I might actually believe you."

Kerr was momentarily surprised, then scowled. "Then you're a lot saner than my daughter. Yet again she's allowed her delusions to—"

"But she's right," Quinn interrupted, shooting the senator a cool stare. "You know something about Layla's death."

"Oh, for the love of God..."

Quinn tilted his head pensively. "Who was it? Sheriff Wilkinson? Are you covering for him in order to have the law under your thumb? Or maybe it was—"

"Get out," Kerr said coldly.

He grinned. "Ah, I'm hitting a nerve. You *do* know who killed that poor girl."

A pair of blue eyes shot daggers at him. "I said get out, Adam."

"In a minute. First I need you to promise you won't do anything to hurt her."

The senator tightened his lips. "I won't commit her. But I will encourage her to leave town."

"Believe me, she won't need much encouragement," Quinn said drily.

Kerr shrugged.

"You truly don't give a damn about her, do you, Senator?" Quinn shook his head in amazement. "She's your daughter."

"She's a nuisance," Kerr snapped. "She always has been."

"You're a selfish son of a bitch, you know that?"

Still shaking his head, Quinn drifted to the door. He paused to toss a final warning over his shoulder. "I'm not kidding. I'll be keeping an eye on you, and if I hear you sent her away, I *will* tell the press what we found in Autumn."

He strode out of the office. Made sure his footsteps were particularly audible as he headed for the elevator. Punching the down button, he waited for the doors to ding open, then ducked into the car, jammed on the "close door" button and ducked right out before the doors slid shut. Walking without making a sound, he crept back toward Kerr's office. He'd left the door ajar, and as he'd predicted, Morgan's father had gone straight to the phone.

Quinn had seen something in the other man's eyes, that same flicker of guilt Morgan glimpsed, but unlike Morgan, he wasn't content with walking away until he knew for sure what happened to Layla Simms.

He flattened his back to the wall and slid toward Kerr's door. The senator spoke in a hushed tone, garbled words that Quinn couldn't quite make out. He waited patiently. Like his daughter, Kerr had a temper, and it wouldn't be long until his voice raised in some sort of outburst.

"Damn it!"

Yep, there it was. Quinn hid a smile.

"I forbid you," the senator was snapping. "It's just a damn necklace, do you hear me? Don't do anything stupid." A pause. "I've covered your ass for ten years. Christ, you won't go to jail. I won't *let* you." Another pause. "Of course I'm thinking about my career! I refuse to lose everything I've worked hard for because you made a stupid mistake ten years ago."

Quinn narrowed his eyes. So the senator had indeed been involved in Layla's death, in the cover-up at least. But who the hell killed her? Jake? Grady Parker?

The answer to the question became painfully clear from the senator's next words.

"The stunt you pulled on that bridge was the last straw. Stay away from your sister, do you understand me?" A long beat. "Goddamn it, Anthony, stay put. I'll take care of it, just like I always do."

Chapter 17

Morgan had never felt lonelier as she wandered around her dark apartment. She was on edge, too restless to sit on the couch, too pissed off to sleep, too angry to eat. She'd taken a shower when she got home, hoping the hot water would ease the tension plaguing her back and shoulders. The shower hadn't helped. Not surprising. How was a shower supposed to make her forget everything that happened the last couple of weeks?

Her father had been involved in her best friend's death. Probably hired someone to drive his own daughter off a bridge.

And Quinn...he was gone.

Talk to him again.

The urgent voice in her head gave her pause. Should she? Quinn was as stubborn as she was, and he'd made it clear he didn't want her back in his life, but could she change his mind? And did she even want to? She'd bared her soul to him so many times the past few days, practically handed him her heart on a silver platter. And each time he'd sent that platter back to the kitchen like a dissatisfied restaurant customer.

Could she really face another rejection?

The sound of the doorbell chimed through the apartment, bringing a surge of hope so strong she would have been embarrassed under any other circumstances. But if Quinn was on the other side of that door, she suspected she would suffer any humiliation if it meant hearing him tell her he loved her.

She smoothed her hair, a self-conscious gesture that unnerved her. *Don't beg,* she ordered herself, then walked to the front door on shaky legs. She'd latched the chain, so the door widened only a few inches, but enough for her to see the visitor wasn't Quinn. Her hope dissipated like smoke from a dying fire. Instead of a pair of familiar green eyes, she found herself looking at a pair of familiar blue ones.

"Hey, Tony, let me get the chain," she sighed, unhooking the latch to let her brother in.

She immediately sensed the agitation spilling out of him. His hands were shoved in the pockets of his black wool coat. Sweat lined his forehead, a damp sheen that suggested he'd either sprinted here from his apartment, which was eight blocks away, or else he was unbelievably nervous.

"You okay?" she asked as she shut the door.

"Not really," Tony mumbled, trailing her into the den.

She wanted to apologize for the clutter—she was a voracious reader and books covered nearly every surface of the cozy room. But Tony seemed oblivious to his surroundings. He shifted, his evident distress making her uneasy.

"Well, you're about to feel worse," she confessed. "I need to tell you something...about Dad...."

"I just spoke to him." Tony met her eyes, his expression resembling that of a betrayed employee who'd just been wrongfully dismissed. "How could you do this to me, Morgan?"

She faltered. "What?"

Her brother began to pace the plush dark red carpet. His eyes were wild. "Why did you have to keep poking around in the case? Why couldn't you leave it alone?"

Pushing aside her hardcover edition of *Great Expectations,* she slowly sank to the couch. "Look, I don't know what Dad told you, but he's lying. He was involved in Layla's death. I don't know whether he killed her, but—"

"He didn't kill her!"

She softened her tone. "I know you don't want to believe it. I didn't, either. But Quinn and I found Mom's necklace in Layla's things. Dad must have given it to her."

Tony abruptly stopped pacing, a wondrous expression filling his eyes. "She kept it," he whispered.

"What?"

But he wasn't looking at her anymore. In fact, he looked as if he were somewhere else, somewhere very far away. "She told me she threw it in the river…I knew she was lying. She wouldn't have done that."

"Who?" She blinked, puzzled. "Are you talking about Mom?"

"Layla." He breathed out the name like he was speaking about a divine God.

An icy fist of fear curled in her belly. "Tony, what are you talking about?" She swallowed. "Oh, God. What did you do?"

His eyes snapped back into focus as he looked at her in outrage. "Me? It wasn't what *I* did. She was going to leave me!"

Morgan's heart began to thud, a sharp staccato that drummed in her ears. She wasn't hearing this. He couldn't possibly be saying any of this. Because if he was, then that meant…

"You killed her," she choked out.

Nausea pooled in her gut like rainwater in a gutter. Tony. *Tony* killed Layla. Tony *killed* Layla.

"She was going to leave me!" His voice came out in a long wail more suited to a child than a thirty-year-old man.

Or an eighteen-year-old boy who'd just lost his mother. That's where she recognized that anguished voice, those tortured words from. *She left me.* Tony had sobbed those words over and over again in the days and weeks following their mother's death.

"You were involved with Layla?" Morgan whispered.

"We were seeing each other for three months." Tony resumed his pacing. "The day she died was our three-month anniversary."

"You mean the day you killed her," Morgan said, nearly gagging on the words.

His eyes blazed. "I couldn't let her leave! She wanted to go back to Jake. Jake, the jock with nothing but air between his ears!"

Morgan shook her head. "Why didn't she tell me about you two? Why didn't you?"

Tony gave a soft, tender smile that made Morgan's blood run cold. "We wanted to keep it a secret. A special secret just between us."

"But Dad knew?"

Consternation lined his forehead. "I had to tell him. After Layla left me, I—"

"After you killed her!" Morgan interrupted heatedly.

"After she left me," he continued, ignoring her outburst, "I called Dad. He came to the woods and helped me take care of everything."

Morgan felt like throwing up. Take care of everything? As in bury a teenage girl's body in the forest and then claim to know nothing about her disappearance? Horror pulsed through her. She couldn't believe this. Her brother killed her best friend, and her father helped cover it up. What the hell kind of people was she related to?

Rage pounded through her blood. Despite the fact that it was Tony who took Layla's life, she suddenly felt like throttling her father. Tony had evidently been more affected by their mother's death than she'd thought, his outward depression shadowing the mental breakdown beneath the surface. He'd snapped when he killed Layla, and what had her father done? Swept the entire mess under the rug in order to protect his precious image. Tony had needed help, damn it! Not a free pass.

"Don't you see?" Tony said, staring at her imploringly. "I couldn't let her leave. Mom left, you know."

Tears stung her eyes when she saw the pout on her brother's face. God, he was a child. A troubled, misguided child who was scared to be alone.

"I know," she murmured, her throat tight. "But I was there. You could have talked to me."

Tony shook his head. "You would have left, too. One day."

She shook her head right back. "You're my brother. I would never abandon you."

A sharp burst of laughter came from his throat. "Maybe not, but you're going to take her away from me, and I can't let that happen."

"Take who away from you?" The fear in her gut deepened, congealing in her blood.

The wild look returned to his eyes. "Caroline!"

"Your girlfriend?" she echoed in confusion. "I'm not trying to take her away from you."

"You want to send me to prison! She's going to leave me if that happens! They always leave me!"

His voice went shrill again. Fighting back tremors of panic, Morgan began to rise from the couch, only to sink right back down when Tony snapped, "Sit down!"

His hands were still concealed in his coat. Morgan suddenly noticed the bulge in his right pocket, and her heart started beating a little faster. "Tony—" she began.

"Shut up." He slowly took one hand out of his pocket, and she saw a flash of silver.

Terror seized her chest. In his hand Tony held a small pistol. If she wasn't mistaken, it had belonged to their mother. Locked up in the safe along with Patricia Kerr's jewelry.

Tony noticed her staring at the gun and smiled. "It was Mom's. I grabbed it from the safe the day I took the necklace."

She swallowed. "You knew the combination?"

"Mom gave it to me when I was eight." He sounded smug, as if to say, *see, she loved me more than you!* "We were very close, you know."

Morgan let out a shaky breath. "Well, why don't you put that away, Tony? We both know you're not going to use it."

His jaw hardened. "Don't pretend to know me! She's the only one who knows me!"

She had no idea which "she" he meant. Their mother. Layla. Caroline. Not that it mattered. It was obvious her brother had snapped years ago, probably long before he murdered Layla Simms. And like an idiot, Morgan hadn't seen it. She'd spent all her time rebelling against their father, fighting for her independence, desperate to get away from the senator and his demands. She saw Tony's devastation following Patricia's death, witnessed his inability to commit to anyone these past ten years, and she'd brushed it off. *He's just picky, can't quite settle down,* she'd always told Quinn.

How ironic, that her father spent years spinning stories to the press about how mentally ill his daughter was, when he had a mentally ill son under his nose the entire time.

"Put the gun away, Tony," she said gently. "Someone could get hurt."

She tried to get up again, but he pointed the weapon at her. *"Sit. Down."*

"Sorry," she said.

Even as she spoke, her gaze was glued to the pistol. It dangled at Tony's side, loosely gripped by his fingers. Could she make a run for it? A part of her refused to believe her brother would ever use that weapon on her, but the strange glaze in his eyes made her wary. She questioned the wisdom of launching herself at him, making a go for the gun, and decided it was too risky.

"I tried to make you stop," he said, looking at her in disapproval. "I didn't want to hurt you, Morgan, but now I have no choice. I can't let her leave me."

Her pulse raced as she echoed, "Make me stop?" Horror slammed into her. "You tried to kill me on the bridge."

"I didn't try to kill you," Tony said with a defensive whine to his voice. "You can swim like a fish. I knew you'd get out of the car. I only wanted to scare you, get you to leave town."

"And last night in my bedroom?" she shot back. "That was you?" He nodded, actually looking remorseful, and his expression brought a rush of fury. "You never left Autumn, did you? You called me, made me believe you were back in the city, but you stayed in town." Betrayal flooded her belly. "How did you know I was alone in my room, that Quinn wasn't with me?"

"The intercom," Tony said with a shrug. "I turned it on before I left."

"And what, you snuck back in later and eavesdropped on us?"

He flushed, suddenly looking annoyed. "You have no right to be angry with me, Morgan. You're the one who opened this can of worms. If you'd just left it alone, everything would be okay now."

"Layla would still be dead," she whispered.

"I couldn't let her leave!"

She was growing sick of his convoluted logic. Her brother had murdered a young girl in cold blood. Her father had covered it up. And no matter how many excuses they tossed her way, she would never forget what either of them had done.

She leveled her gaze at Tony. She felt like shouting at him, throwing something, but she kept her voice calm as she gestured to the gun in his hands and asked, "What exactly are you planning to do with that? Are you going to shoot me, big brother?"

He frowned. "Of course not."

She arched a brow. "No?"

"No, you're going to shoot yourself."

Morgan went speechless. Time seemed to halt. She stared at the fierce look in Tony's eyes, and realized he was dead serious.

Taking a step toward her, he carelessly waved the gun in the air. "Another suicide attempt," he said softly. "Only this time you won't fail."

"I'm not shooting myself," she said through clenched teeth.

"That's how it'll look to the cops." Tony gave her a grim look. "Get the pad of paper from the desk, Morgan."

Her entire body went cold, her veins icy with fear. Oh, God, he was insane. He actually meant to kill her and make it look like a suicide. "No," she said.

He shrugged and walked over to the desk himself. "Fine." He grabbed a pad of paper and a pen, then placed them both on the wooden coffee table in front of her.

"Start writing," he ordered.

Morgan swallowed, searching her mind for a way out of this. She could lunge at him, but chances were, the gun would go off in the struggle. No matter what he'd done to Layla, she didn't want her brother hurt. It was painstakingly apparent that he needed serious psychiatric help.

She suddenly longed for Quinn. If he were here, he'd know exactly how to handle Tony, how to diffuse the time bomb ticking in the room. But Quinn was gone. Probably on his way to Panama or Colombia or who knew where. He didn't want her in his life.

She bit back a hysterical laugh as her gaze landed on the gun pointed at her. Well, looked like Quinn might get his wish. Any second now she might truly be out of his life. For good.

Stall, a voice whispered in her head.

Ah, the old stalling cliché. Keep the psycho talking. Play along until you figured out a plan. Too bad Tony looked like he was through with talking. Impatience creased his face, and he was tapping his foot like a customer at the end of the longest checkout line at the grocery store.

"Start writing!" he snapped, wagging the gun again.

"What do you want me to write?" she finally asked, blinking back the tears.

Tony gave a contemplative slant of the head, then said, "Start with, *Dear Dad, I can't do this anymore.*"

Drawing in a wobbly breath, Morgan picked up the pen.

She was all right. He was just overreacting, Quinn tried to convince himself as he steered the car away from the senate building. He'd tried reaching Morgan on her cell to let her know what he'd just discovered, but he'd been bumped over to voice mail. Then he'd remembered her phone had been confiscated in the psych ward, so he'd dialed her apartment and got the machine there, too. For a moment he'd been tempted to call the police, but he didn't want to alert them about Tony, not until he told Morgan.

Why wasn't she picking up her phone, damn it?

He merged into traffic and almost immediately found himself at a red light, which only gave him more time to imagine all kinds of not-so-pleasant scenarios. The most terrifying one involved him walking into Morgan's apartment to find her dead on the floor.

No, that was absurd. Tony wouldn't harm his sister.

Would he?

The question had been gnawing a hole in his gut since the second he heard Senator Kerr say Tony's name on the phone. Would Tony hurt his own sister? That he couldn't quite answer a definite no to that scared the hell out of him.

The light ahead flicked to green, and his foot shook on the pedal as he accelerated. He was worried. Uneasy. Frankly, even a little terrified. The senator had told Tony that Morgan found the necklace.

Quinn had never killed anyone in cold blood, but it wasn't hard to put himself in Tony's shoes. Tony would be panicking just about now. He'd probably slammed into Morgan on that bridge, probably broken in last night, not to mention all the break-ins ten years ago. The guy was desperate to cover his tracks, to tie up loose ends. And Morgan was a whopper of a loose end.

To hell with it. He'd been heading for a hotel to spend the night in, but at the last second, Quinn yanked on the wheel and pulled a U-turn that made the tires screech and elicited angry honks from other cars on the road. He had to talk to her in person, to make sure she was all right. His instincts were simply misfiring, that's all.

As he sped toward Morgan's place, he tried hard not to imagine the worst. Morgan was almost certainly fine. Angry as hell at her father, who she believed had something to do with Layla's death, but in danger? Nah. She couldn't be. He would stroll into the apartment, find her safe but pissed off and tell her what he'd learned about Tony. He'd convince her to turn her brother in, and then he'd…

He'd what?

Leave her again?

His fingers tightened around the steering wheel. Damn it.

What was he supposed to do? Ever since Morgan walked back into his life, the entire world felt off-kilter. He'd been doing just fine without her. He had his job, the men he worked with, the opportunity to travel all over the world.

He didn't need Morgan. Didn't need anyone.

You're a coward. Morgan's accusation buzzed through his brain. He tried to shut out her voice, but it continued to hover in his mind. She was wrong. He wasn't scared of being with her again. He simply wasn't interested.

So why are you rushing to make sure she's okay?

Duty. Friendship. Because it was the right thing to do.

The voice in his head didn't seem overly convinced by his reasoning. Fortunately, he reached Morgan's low-rise before the voice started up again.

*Un*fortunately, a familiar tan sedan sat by the curb in front of Morgan's building.

Tony was here.

A vise of dread clamped around Quinn's heart. He parked behind Tony's car and jumped out of the SUV. Hurrying through the glass doors at the entrance, he bypassed the elevator and headed for the stairwell, because in his experience elevators were too damn slow. He pulled his gun from his waistband as he sprinted up the stairs to the second floor. Morgan's apartment was at the end of the long corridor. Quinn slowed his pace, inching down the plush carpeting beneath his feet toward Morgan's apartment.

The door was closed, but a gentle tug on the handle showed it wasn't locked. Holding his breath, Quinn slid inside. Nobody greeted him in the front hall, but he could hear the murmur of voices drifting out from the den. The small apartment was cloaked in darkness, save for the shaft of light coming from the living room doorway.

He moved toward the light without making a solitary sound. His pulse surprisingly steady, his body relaxed, his mind void of emotion. This was what he did. Crept in the shadows. Eliminated the enemy. He'd been trained for this. Often enjoyed it.

But he wasn't enjoying a damn thing at the moment. As he got closer to the doorway, he heard Morgan's throaty voice. "No one will believe I wrote this," she was protesting.

"Keep writing," came her brother's sharp reply. "Say *I'm sorry for all the pain I've caused everyone.*"

Quinn flattened himself against the wall next to the door frame, then, ever so carefully, cocked his head to peek inside. For the first time since he'd entered the apartment, his pulse sped up. Morgan sat on the couch, a pad of paper in her hands. Looming over her was Tony.

And pointed at her forehead was a small, but very lethal, pistol.

Chapter 18

Quinn swallowed the lump of fury that rose in his throat. He wanted to hurl himself into the room. Heave himself at Tony, knock the gun out of his hand. Or even easier, simply step into the doorway and put a bullet in the back of Tony Kerr's head. But he kept the volatile urges in check. Any sort of ambush was liable to get Morgan killed.

"They won't believe it," she said again. "This doesn't sound like me."

Tony's responding shout was heavy with aggravation. "Just do it!"

"Fine, but I'm just saying…"

She sounded scared, but in control. A burst of pride filled Quinn's chest. Any other woman—hell, any man—would have been freaking out just about now. Stay calm when someone had a gun aimed at your head? Not many people could do it. But Morgan…God, she was so damn strong. In some ways, a hell of a lot stronger than him.

"Now sign it," Tony ordered.

Quinn could practically feel her hesitation. He didn't blame her, either. Evidently Tony was forcing her to write a suicide note, which meant that the moment she signed her name, it was all over.

A long silence descended, finally broken by Tony saying, "Good girl." Regret dripped from his voice. "I'm so sorry about this, Morgan. You understand why I have to do this, right?"

Quinn's muscles tensed as he heard Tony's footsteps, most likely moving closer to Morgan. He tightened his grip on the gun.

"She'll leave me if the truth comes out."

"But I'm expendable?" came Morgan's embittered retort.

"Don't say that." Tony sounded genuinely remorseful. "I love you, Mor. But you're the one who screwed everything up." A beat of silence. "Close your eyes, okay? It'll be over soon."

Like hell it would.

Quinn propelled into action. He swiftly entered the room and fixed the weapon on the sandy-haired man. "Put the gun down, Tony," he said sternly.

Tony spun around, a stunned expression on his face. The surprise quickly faded into an irritated scowl.

"Why are you here?" Tony demanded. "Why can't everyone just *leave this alone?*"

"Put the gun down," Quinn repeated. "You don't want to do this, Tony. You don't want to hurt your sister."

Morgan's brother stared at him in disbelief. "You shouldn't care what happens to her, Quinn. She left you!"

Quinn's lips tightened. "Actually, I left her."

He'd been doing his best to not look at Morgan, but he couldn't help it now. His gaze swept over to her, and his heart squeezed when he noticed the tears sticking to her thick eyelashes. Haphazard strands of golden hair had fallen from her loose ponytail to frame her face. She was pale. Looked exhausted and scared and concerned—and so incredibly beautiful his eyes hurt from looking at her.

And she was his. She'd stolen his heart the day, no, the *second,* they'd met, and for the past two years he'd been kidding himself. He wasn't over her. Never had been. Never would be. That heart she'd stolen, well, she owned it now, and she always would.

"You left because she didn't give a damn about you," Tony replied. A knowing look crossed his face. "Layla didn't give a damn about me, too."

"So you decided to take a rock and smash her head in?" Quinn spat out despite the warning voice telling him to keep quiet.

Tony's face turned a bright shade of crimson. "It was an accident."

"Sure didn't look that way on the coroner's report. Six fractures to the skull." Quinn made a tsk sound with his tongue. "Sounds more like old-fashioned murder to me."

From the corner of his eye, he saw Morgan's face pleading with him to stop. *Don't bait him,* she mouthed. But Quinn knew exactly what he was doing. As he spoke, he moved ever so nearer to the other man, until they were standing only a couple of feet apart.

"Don't come any closer," Tony ordered, panic flooding his gaze.

"You murdered that girl," Quinn said softly. "You murdered her, buried her in the woods, and put it out of your mind."

"Shut up!"

"And now you're about to murder your own sister."

"I said *shut up!*"

Quinn took another step forward. "Tony, you need help."

"Don't move!" The gun shook wildly in Tony's hands.

Quinn's peripheral vision caught Morgan beginning to rise from the couch, but he ordered her with a glare to stay put. She got the message loud and clear, and sank back down.

"You've made some terrible mistakes," Quinn went on. "But that doesn't mean your life is over. There were obviously extenuating circumstances, Tony. Any judge would see that."

"Judge?" Tony echoed. His eyes widened. "There won't be a judge! I can't go to jail! Caroline will leave me if I—"

Quinn pounced, ramming his shoulder into Tony's chest. The sudden attack caused Tony to drop the pistol. As the gun fell onto the carpet, Tony fell, too, the force of Quinn's blow sending him sprawling backward. But the other man took Quinn with him, his fingers clutching the hem of Quinn's sweater. As his equilibrium failed him, Quinn lost his grip on his own gun. The two men hit the floor.

A fist connected with Quinn's left cheekbone. He fought back, landing a left hook in the corner of Tony's mouth. Blood spurted from Tony's lip, eliciting a strangled shout. Quinn was amazed by Tony's strength as they struggled on the carpet. He pinned the other man down, only to have the tables turn and find himself flat on his back. Tony landed another punch, then heaved himself off Quinn, one arm outstretched in a desperate attempt to reach the gun that had been pushed under the coffee table.

Adrenaline surged through Quinn's body. Tony's last punch had him seeing stars, but he fought the dizzying rush and launched himself at the other man again. Unfortunately, Tony had already gotten his hands on the pistol. With a quick roll to the side, Quinn dove for his own gun, his hand connecting with it at the same moment Tony lifted his pistol and pointed it at Morgan, who was making a mad dash to the living room doorway.

Quinn watched in horror as Tony aimed the weapon at his sister, but his hesitation only lasted a split second. As Tony's finger tightened on the trigger, Quinn unloaded two bullets into the other man's chest.

The roar of the gunshots reverberated through the room, leaving a shrill ringing in Quinn's ears.

"What…" Tony slowly looked down at his chest, watching in disbelief as two crimson patches bloomed on his pale blue shirt. As the color drained from his face, he let go of the pistol and fell onto his side. Blood poured out of his wounds and stained Morgan's carpet.

Quinn immediately went to Tony's side, tucked the fallen gun in his waistband, but kept his own weapon trained on the injured man. "Call 911," he barked at Morgan, who stood like a terrified deer in the doorway.

"Oh, my God," she whispered, her breathing coming out in sharp bursts. "Oh, God, is he okay?"

"911, Morgan!"

Her footsteps were frantic as she dashed for the cordless phone on the desk and called the police. Quinn heard her talking to the dispatcher, but he couldn't focus on what she said. Instead, he looked at Tony, whose entire face was white as a sheet. He was losing blood fast.

"She left me," Tony whispered, staring up him in astonishment.

"Don't talk," Quinn said quietly.

He quickly removed his jacket, balled up the sleeve and pressed it to the gaping wounds on Tony's chest. But he had a feeling no amount of pressure would make this better. The color continued draining from Tony's face, as fast as the blood seeping out of the two bullet holes in his chest.

Morgan rushed over to them and dropped to her knees. Her eyes widened when she saw the unsettling amount of blood on her carpet. "Is he going to be okay?" she said anxiously.

Quinn shot her a sideways glance. Gave an imperceptible shake of the head.

Tears filled her eyes. "Oh, God." Immediately, she added her own hands to her brother's chest, pressing Quinn's jacket into the wounds to stanch the bleeding. "Tony, can you hear me?"

Her brother's eyelids fluttered. "Mom?" he breathed out.

Morgan swallowed. "No, it's—" She gasped as Quinn squeezed her knee hard. She glanced over in confusion, saw his nod, and a glimmer of sorrow lit her blue eyes. She nodded back, then turned to her brother again. "Yes, it's me."

Tony's eyes were completely out of focus as he looked up at her, but the reverence in his voice was unmistakable. "Are you going to take care of me?"

"Yes, sweetheart," Morgan choked out. "I'm going to take care of you."

"Mom?"

"Yes, Tony?"

"I'm sorry," he whispered.

The chest that had been rising and falling beneath their fingers became motionless. Quinn stifled a heavy sigh. Damn it. This wasn't how he'd wanted things to turn out. Tony might have been a murderer, but he was Morgan's brother. And he had needed professional help, not a death sentence.

Beside him, Morgan let out an anguished sob. "He's gone." She lifted her bloodstained hands and stared at them in dismay.

Quinn's heart ached for her. Yet as he glanced at Tony Kerr's still body, he couldn't muster up any regret for what he'd done. Tony would have shot Morgan. He would have *killed* her. And there was nothing more important to Quinn in the world than protecting the woman by his side.

Because he loved her. God help him, he loved her.

Sirens shrieked from a distance, getting closer, but neither of them made any move to get up. Quinn slowly drew Morgan into his arms, where she cried over her brother's body until the police finally arrived and pulled her away.

"You ready to go?"

Morgan turned at the sound of Quinn's voice. She'd been leaning against the wall in the lobby of the metropolitan police department, waiting for Quinn's interrogation to end. Her own questioning had lasted forty-five minutes, during which she'd told the detective in charge about everything she'd discovered. Including the fact that her father helped her brother cover up Layla Simms's death.

Quinn was taken into a neighboring room, but the cops kept him for a full hour after she'd been released. Probably because he was the one who pulled the trigger. The one who killed her brother.

Tears stung her eyes as she watched him approach. His jacket, soaked with Tony's blood, had been taken into evidence, so he wore only a black button-down over a gray T-shirt that stretched across his broad chest. There were bloodstains on his jeans, but Morgan forced herself not to dwell on those. Instead, she focused on his deep green eyes, the thick stubble sweeping across his jaw, the hesitant expression creasing his handsome face.

He killed her brother tonight.

And yet if he hadn't, Tony would have killed *her*.

Grief and relief warred inside her. She had no idea what to feel. She wanted to mourn her brother. But how could she not be relieved? She was safe. Quinn was safe. If Quinn hadn't gotten there when he did…she forced away the memory of Tony's feral eyes and the frantic way he'd waved that gun around. She still couldn't believe her own brother had planned to kill her.

She managed a weak smile. "They didn't charge you with anything?"

Quinn shook his head. "They decided it was self-defense."

Morgan swallowed a lump of sorrow. "You saved my life."

Rather than answering, Quinn shrugged out of his button-down and held it out. "Put this on. It's cold outside."

"Thank you." She slid her arms into the long sleeves of the shirt, immediately surrounded by the lingering warmth from his body and the heady scent of him. The cops hadn't given her time to grab a coat when they left the apartment.

When her brother's body had been rolled out on a stretcher, covered with a black tarp...

She pushed away the grisly image and followed Quinn out the front doors. They descended the steps of the police station, pausing on the sidewalk. The sky was inky black, the night breeze carrying with it a chill that made Morgan grateful for Quinn's shirt. He, on the other hand, wore only a T-shirt.

"You'll catch a cold," she said. "Let's hail a cab."

Despite the late hour—it was nearly midnight—Indiana Avenue was bustling. Cars whizzed past them, brake lights leaving streaks of red as the vehicles sped by. Morgan moved to the edge of the curb, spotted an approaching taxi and prepared to raise her hand.

A warm hand stopped her from hailing the cab. "Let's walk for a bit," came Quinn's gravelly voice.

She turned to him in surprise. "Aren't you cold?"

"No. I need the fresh air at the moment."

She wondered if he could still smell it, too. The coppery scent of Tony's blood. It was clogged in her nostrils. Made her want to throw up.

"Good idea," she murmured.

They started walking. In silence. Morgan didn't know how long they walked, how far, and she didn't particularly care. Tonight had been...devastating. She just wanted to walk, and walk, and walk, until maybe she could eventually forget it all.

But Quinn didn't let her forget.

"They'll be bringing charges up against your father," he began softly. "As an accessory to murder."

"I know. The detective told me the same thing." She sighed. "They won't stick, though. The only thing tying my dad to the crime is my statement. Tony's—" she swallowed "—dead, so he can't corroborate it."

"He'll lose his seat, though," Quinn said.

"Probably. The senate won't be thrilled to find out he's a suspect in a murder investigation, however old it may be." She shrugged. "Most likely he'll be forced to resign. We both know my dad won't put himself through the expulsion proceedings. He'll try to sweep the entire mess under the rug."

They reached a small park, which consisted of a couple of benches, a drinking fountain and some stone statues of people Morgan didn't recognize. She made a move to keep walking, but Quinn touched her arm. "Let's sit for a while."

With a nod, she trailed after him. They sat on one of the metal benches. Glancing over, she noticed the goose bumps dotting his bare arms, but didn't comment on it. He obviously wanted to sit, despite the fact that the temperature seemed to be dropping in degrees by the second.

"Will you forgive him?" Quinn asked suddenly.

"For helping my brother cover up my best friend's death?" She blinked back tears. "I'm not sure I can."

"He's still your father."

Morgan stared at him in surprise. "Since when has that made a difference? You've never liked him, and he's always been my father."

His green eyes flickered indefinably. "I..." He cleared his throat. "I never thought about...about what it meant."

"What are you talking about?"

"The word *family*." He gave her a sad look. "I never had any, so I couldn't understand why you put up with him, in spite of the way he treated you, the crappy things he did. I didn't get it. Until tonight."

Morgan said nothing. She had the feeling they were on the verge of...something. And the last thing she wanted to do was ruin it.

"You were crying," he went on, his voice thick with emotion. "When Tony died, you were crying. And that's when I realized it. No matter what he did, no matter how unforgivable his actions, he was still your brother. Your family."

"Yes," she whispered in agreement.

"It's the same with your father, isn't it? He's... Damn, Morgan, he's despicable, but...he's your family."

"Yes."

Quinn fell silent again. She waited for him to continue, but he didn't. He just sat there, his long legs stretched out in front of him, his taut biceps covered with gooseflesh, his gaze straight ahead.

Morgan breathed in, then exhaled, her breath a wispy white cloud that hung in the air. "Are you staying in a hotel tonight?" she finally asked, unable to bear the silence.

"Yeah," he said.

"And tomorrow? Are you leaving town?"

Another "yeah."

She ignored the painful squeeze of her heart. "Where to?"

"I'm not sure yet. Murphy and the guys probably finished up the Caracas job. Not sure what the next gig will be." He released a puff of cold air. "Hopefully somewhere warm."

"See, you *are* cold!" she accused. She jumped to her feet. "C'mon, let's find a cab and get you—"

"I want you to come with me."

Her gaze flew to his. "What?"

"I want you to come with me." A vulnerable crack trembled in his husky voice. "Will you?"

She sank right back down, her butt landing on the bench with a thud. Evidently she was more exhausted than she'd thought. Exhaustion caused auditory hallucinations, right?

"Morgan?"

She just stared at him.

"Will you come with me?"

Blinking out of whatever trance she'd fallen into, she swallowed down her disbelief. "Am I hearing things, or did you actually ask me to go with you?"

His lips quirked. "You're not hearing things."

"But...why?" She shook her head, still not understanding where any of this was coming from. "For God's sake, Quinn, I practically recited an entire scene from *Jerry Maguire,* told you I loved you, how I'd always put you first, and you..." A stab of pain went through her. "You said you weren't interested. What the hell changed?"

Remorse flooded his gaze. "Everything," he said simply.

That one word was laced with such passion she had trouble breathing for a moment.

"Tonight, when I saw that gun aimed at you..." He stared at her in agony. "I imagined it going off, I *saw* the bullet entering your body, *felt* your heart stopping, and...and I knew if it actually happened, my heart would stop, too."

Tears pricked her eyelids. Her chest suddenly felt tight, her heart expanding, filling with warmth and love and...hope.

"I can't live without you, Morgan," he choked out. "I tried, for two damn years, and it didn't work. I need you with me, sweetheart."

A single tear slid down her cheek. He instantly leaned toward her and brushed it away, his touch so gentle she only began to cry in fervor.

"You were right," he added. "I didn't forgive you." Through the sheen of tears, she saw the shame in his eyes.

"I told myself I did, because really, I needed to get over you, and holding on to the anger and resentment would have stopped me from doing that. But I still blamed you. For constantly letting your father interfere with our life. For canceling our wedding. I didn't understand how you could possibly do any of that, and yet claim to love me."

He stroked her cheek, adding, "I forgot what it was like to have a family. And I get it now, why you made the choices you did."

"I was wrong," she whispered.

"We both were," he corrected. His green eyes darkened. "I should have never left you."

Her tears ceased, but emotions continued swirling inside of her, gathering, growing, circling her heart. When he walked out of her life, she'd thought it was for good. She'd never been happier to be wrong in her entire life.

"So, that second chance you mentioned…" He smiled faintly. "I'm game. Are you?"

She smiled back, wiping her eyes with the sleeve of Quinn's shirt. "Hell, yes."

Sliding closer, Quinn wrapped one arm around her waist. His other arm lifted to stroke her hair. He pushed a few wayward strands away from her face, and then his mouth came down on hers. The kiss sent a thrill through her body, sizzling down her spine and settling deep in her core. When his tongue licked at her lips, she whimpered, opening her mouth to grant him access. His tongue slid inside, dueling with hers, exploring every crevice.

She ran her fingers through his dark hair, pulling him closer to her. Moaning, she rubbed her breasts against the hard ripples of his chest. He gave an answering groan and deepened the kiss, claiming her mouth with urgency.

When they finally broke apart, they were both panting. Quinn dragged his finger along the line of her jaw, smiling again. "So…will you?"

It took a second for her brain to function again.

"Will I what?" she said breathlessly.

"Come with me."

"Where?"

The smile widened, revealing his perfectly straight white teeth. "Anywhere we want. Wherever my job takes us, wherever yours takes us. Just promise me you'll never leave my side, baby."

Her heart did a little jumping jack. "Only if you promise the same."

"Oh, I promise." His voice was thick. "I will never leave your side again, Morgan. In fact, I think we should get married. Right now."

She grinned. "Oh, really? Don't you think you should propose first?"

"I proposed two years ago." He shot her a roguish look. "There's no statute of limitations on proposals. So since you said yes the first time around, it still counts."

A laugh tickled her throat. "Okay, so you want me to leave town with you, you want me to marry you…anything else?"

"Just one more thing."

She arched one eyebrow. "Which is?"

"I want to tell you I love you."

A rush of heat seared her entire body. That she was able to breathe normally was nothing short of a miracle. She hadn't heard those three words leave his sexy mouth in two very long years. Hearing them now infused her with intense joy that left her utterly speechless.

"I'm not sure you heard me. Should I say it again?" he teased.

She nodded.

"I love you." He dipped his head and pressed a tender kiss to her lips. Then he pulled back and said those magical words once more. "I love you, Morgan."

Finally regaining her capacity for speech, she met his gaze. Saw all the love she felt reflecting back at her in his deep green eyes.

She opened her mouth, her voice heavy with emotion. "I love you, too…Adam."

Epilogue

Six months later

"**M**organ, are you out here?"

Quinn strode outside and searched the private stretch of warm, white sand for his wife. He spotted her sitting on an oversize towel a few yards away, shielded by a colorful red-and-green beach umbrella and sipping on a glass of what looked like pink lemonade.

What the hell?

He'd just gotten in from Panama, and broken every traffic law in order to get to the beach house they'd been renting for the past month. Morgan had left a cryptic message on his voice mail, something about a change of plans and possible complications. He'd immediately picked up on the note of anxiety in her voice, so he bid goodbye to his team at the airstrip and sped home like a maniac. And what did he find? His wife relaxing on the beach.

"What's going on?" he demanded as he reached her towel.

The sun sat high in the middle of the clear blue sky. It was bright as hell, and Morgan was squinting as she tilted her head up at him. Her face was tanned and radiant, her body covered by a yellow bikini that rose high on her sleek thighs and barely covered her breasts.

They'd been living in Costa Rica for six months now, though the beach house in Tamarindo Bay was merely a home base of sorts. They came and went during the past months. To Brazil, where Morgan had chased a story. Johannesburg, where Quinn had another close call—what was with his bad luck in Johannesburg?!—during an extraction. And of course, Fiji, just for fun.

Despite all the traveling, they kept tabs on what was going on in the States. D.C., in particular. The most recent news had been Senator Edward Kerr's resignation from the United States Senate. Morgan had phoned him with her condolences, but neither she nor Quinn felt too sympathetic about the senator's exit from the senate, because luckily for Senator Kerr—and unluckily for the Simms family—no charges had been brought up against him for his role in Layla's death. His part in the crime would forever go unpunished, and it was something Morgan was still having a tough time accepting.

"Why do you look so worried?" she asked, setting down her glass on the rickety little table she'd dragged out onto the beach their first day there.

"Because of you," he said darkly. "What was that message about? Complications? Change of plans? What on earth were you talking about?"

She gave a shrug. "I just wanted to let you know we might need to alter some of the plans we made."

"Such as?"

"The trip to Australia. Oh, and definitely the one to Russia we had planned for the winter—I'm dropping the story about the underage prostitutes. I should have been freelancing all along." The dimple in her chin popped out. "I like choosing what to write, and scrapping stories when needed."

Quinn frowned. "Why do you need to drop the Russia piece?"

Another innocent little shrug. "It's not safe to travel in the third trimester."

His heart nearly stopped.

Morgan grinned.

"Did you just say what I think you said?" he blurted.

"Yep." She let out a mock sigh. "You knocked me up."

Quinn stood frozen for a moment, while the hot sun burned a hole in the back of his head. When his brain resumed its ability to function, a grin spread over his face and he dropped to his knees, sending grains of sand flying in all directions.

He yanked Morgan into his arms and kissed her with fervor. "Are you sure?" he said, pulling back.

Her entire face glowed with delight. "The doctor confirmed it yesterday. I'm three months along."

Tiny bursts of joy went off in his body. He quickly did the math. "So this October…" He looked at her in wonder. "Do you know if it's a boy or girl?"

She wrinkled her forehead, as if the question was utterly absurd. "Of course I know. The suspense would have killed me."

He couldn't help but laugh. "Right, I should've known."

Morgan cocked her head, and a strand of blond hair came free of her ponytail and fell into her eyes. She pushed it away and said, "Do you want to know?"

He only hesitated for a moment. It would be nice to be surprised. On the other hand, his motto was be prepared. And he wouldn't know what color to paint the damn nursery if he waited until October.

He gave a brisk nod. "Okay, tell me."

Morgan's eyes twinkled. "Girl."

Quinn's heart squeezed with emotion. He could already see his daughter's face in his mind, the spitting image of her beautiful mother. He suddenly let out a groan, abruptly got to his feet and took two steps.

"Where are you going?" Morgan demanded, looking perplexed.

He sighed. "To buy a shotgun. That way I'll have it on hand when our baby girl starts dating."

Morgan let out a melodic laugh. "Oh, quit being melodramatic. That won't happen for at least, what? Thirteen years?"

"Try thirty," he said stiffly.

She laughed again, then beckoned at him with one delicate hand. "Stop sulking and get back over here, Adam. We still have a lot more celebrating to do."

With a grin, he sank onto the sand again and wrapped his arms around his gorgeous wife. As their lips met, he knew without a doubt that he'd finally found what he'd been yearning for his entire life. Love. Happiness. Acceptance. Family.

* * * * *

*See below for a sneak peek from our classic
Harlequin® Romance® line.*

Introducing DADDY BY CHRISTMAS by Patricia Thayer.

MIA caught sight of Jarrett when he walked into the open lobby. It was hard not to notice the man. In a charcoal business suit with a crisp white shirt and striped tie covered by a dark trench coat, he looked more Wall Street than small-town Colorado.

Mia couldn't blame him for keeping his distance. He was probably tired of taking care of her.

Besides, why would a man like Jarrett McKane be interested in her? Why would he want to take on a woman expecting a baby? Yet he'd done so many things for her. He'd been there when she'd needed him most. How could she not care about a man like that?

Heart pounding in her ears, she walked up behind him. Jarrett turned to face her. "Did you get enough sleep last night?"

"Yes, thanks to you," she said, wondering if he'd thought about their kiss. Her gaze went to his mouth, then she quickly glanced away. "And thank you for not bringing up my meltdown."

Jarrett couldn't stop looking at Mia. Blue was definitely her color, bringing out the richness of her eyes.

"What meltdown?" he said, trying hard to focus on what she was saying. "You were just exhausted from lack of sleep and worried about your baby."

He couldn't help remembering how, during the night, he'd kept going in to watch her sleep. How strange was that? "I hope you got enough rest."

She nodded. "Plenty. And you're a good neighbor for

coming to my rescue."

He tensed. Neighbor? *What neighbor kisses you like I did?* "That's me, just the full-service landlord," he said, trying to keep the sarcasm out of his voice. He started to leave, but she put her hand on his arm.

"Jarrett, what I meant was you went beyond helping me." Her eyes searched his face. "I've asked far too much of you."

"Did you hear me complain?"

She shook her head. "You should. I feel like I've taken advantage."

"Like I said, I haven't minded."

"And I'm grateful for everything…"

Grasping her hand on his arm, Jarrett leaned forward. The memory of last night's kiss had him aching for another. "I didn't do it for your gratitude, Mia."

Gorgeous tycoon Jarrett McKane has never believed in Christmas—but he can't help being drawn to soon-to-be-mom Mia Saunders! Christmases past were spent alone…and now Jarrett may just have a fairy-tale ending for all his Christmases future!

Available December 2010, only from Harlequin® Romance®.

HARLEQUIN®

A Romance

FOR EVERY MOOD™

Spotlight on

Classic

Quintessential, modern love stories
that are romance at its finest.

See the next page
to enjoy a sneak peek from
the Harlequin® Romance series.

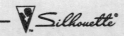

SPECIAL EDITION

USA TODAY BESTSELLING AUTHOR

MARIE FERRARELLA

BRINGS YOU ANOTHER
HEARTWARMING STORY FROM

When Lilli McCall disappeared on him
after he proposed, Kullen Manetti swore
never to fall in love again. Eight years later
Lilli is back in his life, threatening to break
down all the walls he's put up to
safeguard his heart.

UNWRAPPING
THE PLAYBOY

*Available December
wherever books are sold.*

REQUEST YOUR FREE BOOKS!

2 FREE NOVELS PLUS 2 FREE GIFTS!

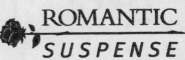

Sparked by Danger, Fueled by Passion.

YES! Please send me 2 FREE Silhouette® Romantic Suspense novels and my 2 FREE gifts (gifts are worth about $10). After receiving them, if I don't wish to receive any more books, I can return the shipping statement marked "cancel." If I don't cancel, I will receive 4 brand-new novels every month and be billed just $4.24 per book in the U.S. or $4.99 per book in Canada. That's a saving of 15% off the cover price! It's quite a bargain! Shipping and handling is just 50¢ per book.* I understand that accepting the 2 free books and gifts places me under no obligation to buy anything. I can always return a shipment and cancel at any time. Even if I never buy another book from Silhouette, the two free books and gifts are mine to keep forever.

240/340 SDN E5Q4

Name	(PLEASE PRINT)	
Address		Apt. #
City	State/Prov.	Zip/Postal Code

Signature (if under 18, a parent or guardian must sign)

Mail to the **Silhouette Reader Service:**

IN U.S.A.: P.O. Box 1867, Buffalo, NY 14240-1867
IN CANADA: P.O. Box 609, Fort Erie, Ontario L2A 5X3

Not valid for current subscribers to Silhouette Romantic Suspense books.

Want to try two free books from another line?
Call 1-800-873-8635 or visit www.morefreebooks.com.

---

* Terms and prices subject to change without notice. Prices do not include applicable taxes. N.Y. residents add applicable sales tax. Canadian residents will be charged applicable provincial taxes and GST. Offer not valid in Quebec. This offer is limited to one order per household. All orders subject to approval. Credit or debit balances in a customer's account(s) may be offset by any other outstanding balance owed by or to the customer. Please allow 4 to 6 weeks for delivery. Offer available while quantities last.

SRS10R